Every is to start somewhere

THE OPIATE MURDERS 3

Vancouver's Pain and Wastings

Justin Sand

For Zack

Justin Sand

FriesenPress

One Printers Way
Altona, MB R0G 0B0
Canada

www.friesenpress.com

Copyright © 2022 by Justin Sand
First Edition — 2022

All rights reserved.

No part of this publication may be reproduced in any form, or by any means, electronic or mechanical, including photocopying, recording, or any information browsing, storage, or retrieval system, without permission in writing from FriesenPress.

Stevie Sand, Photographer

ISBN
978-1-03-914801-7 (Hardcover)
978-1-03-914800-0 (Paperback)
978-1-03-914802-4 (eBook)

1. FICTION, CRIME

Distributed to the trade by The Ingram Book Company

1

March 5, 1993

BRIAN DAXON JEFFRIES FELT THE BLINDING HALOGEN BEFORE HE EVEN opened his eyes. All he could smell was burnt rubber and that taste of phosphorus that lingers on well past its inception. His arms were tingling and weak. Sweat beaded off his forehead. He could feel the restriction below his waist; he was held in place by something foreign. His throat was dry, and his thoughts were scattered as he blinked rapidly to gain focus. The first thing he could see, he couldn't quite make out. As it came into focus, his eyes widened to meet the sight. His right leg was suspended at a forty-five degree angle in a cast with pins sticking out of it with round metallic circles holding them in place. He closed his eyes again and drifted off. He was just sixteen years old.

When he came to again, two nurses were standing over him. One of them quickly left when they both saw that he was awake. The back of his head was hot, and he kept scratching it against a grainy pillow, which made him even more uncomfortable. As he forced himself to reach for it, it was taken by one of the nurses and adjusted. Brian opened his eyes again, and a straw was put into his mouth. He sipped relentlessly for sustenance as his eyes darted back and forth to examine the eyes that were staring at him.

A middle-aged man in a white coat stepped forward holding a clip board. "Hello, Brian. My name is Dr. Fisher."

Brian nodded. His eyes were held open by the smallest thread.

"You've been in an accident, Brian," the doctor said, as Brian looked at his leg again with greater attention. "Do you remember anything?" the doctor asked as

Brian's mind searched for an answer. "I was on the way to soccer practice when a car hit us," Brian said to his own surprise. His voice didn't seem to be his own.

"Yes, that's correct. Do you remember anything else?"

Brian shook his head.

The doctor took a deep breath and said, "Brian, you were hit by a car that flipped the vehicle you were in five times. You were pinned beneath the road and the car for some time before the jaws of life were used to cut you from the wreck. You sustained a midshaft right femur fracture, which we have pinned and plated, as you can see. You suffered a left posterior hip dislocation, which has caused serious nerve damage. Your right leg was broken in three places. Your upper body was left mostly unharmed except for your arm and the back of your head that have mild burns that will heal in time. You are very lucky to be alive."

Just then, Brian realized that something was missing, something that he couldn't name, and then he said it without thinking. "Where's my dad?"

The doctor looked back at Brian and put his chart down. "Brian, your dad was killed instantly. You were air-lifted here to St. Paul's from Victoria. I'm sorry."

Brian lay there for a few seconds and felt faint. His eyes closed, and he never wanted them to open again.

2

April 23, 2013

CASSIDY NEWMAN SAT ON THE STEPS OF THE POLICE STATION, GATHERING her notes and sipping her first cup of coffee. She was twenty-three years old, and this was her first real assignment for the newspaper, where she had been getting coffee for people for the last three years. She had a journalism degree from Simon Fraser University, which didn't carry much weight. She was a small fish in a big pond.

She was dressed casually, with blue jeans, Chuck Taylor shoes, and a blue sweater underneath her jean jacket. Her shoulder-length, brown hair was held in place by a light blue toque. Cassidy wore little makeup, and she ignored the eyes of the uniformed police officers that looked her over as they passed by. She didn't really notice the attention she got when she walked around, but today, she would keep her glances to herself it was important to be inconspicuous. Beauty can be a liability as much as an asset, especially in journalism. She needed to be taken seriously.

Just then, an unmarked cruiser pulled up, and the window opened. "You Cassidy?" a woman said from the passenger seat.

"Yes," Cassidy replied as she stood up and gathered her things.

"Hop in the back," the woman said as Cassidy climbed in the cruiser, and they sped away. "My name is Detective Anderson, and this is Detective Lancer," she said back to Cassidy through the plexiglass.

Cassidy studied the man driving for a minute. He was tall, with a military-grade haircut and solid, square shoulders. He wore a T-shirt and jeans, which Cassidy found surprising for a detective, but Detective Anderson seemed underdressed too. Anderson had on khaki pants, a black blazer over a white shirt, and was wearing a New York Yankees cap. She had a soft brown complexion like she was from the Caribbean Islands. Cassidy guessed Anderson was in her thirties, and she definitely wore more makeup than Cassidy would have expected. Cassidy felt more relaxed because of this, except for the plexiglass, it was a pretty casual environment.

"So, we got the memo, as in our staff sergeant told us to give you a tour. What would you like to see?" Anderson asked, after they had traveled a few more blocks.

Detective Lancer twitched his shoulders at the high-pitched sound that came out of the radio, and quickly turned the static down.

"Well, I'm here to do a story about the rise in police detentions under the Mental Health Act since the closing of Riverview Mental Hospital last year," Cassidy said, sitting up straighter as she said it.

Lancer put his head to the side like he was cracking his neck to meet the comment. He then coughed and rotated his grip on the steering wheel. Anderson glanced at him and then looked off out the window. "Well, it all started a long time before they closed the Riverview," she said. Since 2010, we have seen a 16% increase in Section 28's of the Mental Health Act. We get about 150 calls a day here in the Downtown Eastside. That's up from eighty-something five years ago, and it's 30% of all emergency calls."

Cassidy already knew all this. That's why she was here, and everybody in the car knew it, she felt. Cassidy picked over her words carefully, trying to remember her training. She wanted them to talk. *She wanted them to open up to her, but how do you do that?* She thought. Cassidy's palms started to sweat; something that she did when she was nervous. She looked out the window at the carts lined up against walls and homeless people shuffling everywhere.

They parked their car at Carnegie Community Center. "I'm also here to ask questions about the overdose deaths involving a new drug named fentanyl," Cassidy asked finally after giving up on waiting and seeing. Cassidy's eyes shot back and forth between the two detectives, as she waited for a response.

"You seeing that?" Lancer said to Anderson.

"Yep," Anderson repeated.

Cassidy searched the windows, looking for what they were talking about. Just then Cassidy saw it just as Lancer jumped from the car and put his hands up in the air. A man was walking in the middle of the street with a knife to his throat.

"Don't think I won't," he repeated as he looked at anyone approaching him. He walked right past Lancer and said, "I've killed, and I'll kill again," as he turned down an adjacent alley.

Anderson turned around and said, "Are you coming or not?" as she jumped out of the car.

Cassidy followed her and Lancer as they tracked the man into the alley. The man with the knife stopped and sat down and started picking his teeth with the knife.

"Have you talked to your mother today, Toney?" Lancer said when he had squared off with the man.

Toney looked up and said, "Why would I talk to her if she is one of them?"

Lancer looked over at Anderson, and she said, "Toney, have you picked up your meds today from Doctor Moral?"

Toney looked at the both of them and said, "I would if you two would stop bothering me."

Lancer laughed and said, "I got a deal for you, Toney. You go pick up your meds, and we will leave you alone, okay?"

"I didn't even do anything you guys are infringing on my rights!" Toney said scratching his head with the knife.

"We're sorry, Toney. Tell the doctor I said 'hi'," Anderson said with a chuckle, and the two of them turned around and walked past Cassidy.

Toney looked Cassidy up and down and said, "You smell like university," and then went back to picking his teeth.

Cassidy turned around and followed the two back to the car. Cassidy was too scared and confused to play it cool, so she just went into it. "You're just going to leave him there with a weapon threatening to harm himself?" she asked awkwardly with her voice breaking in the middle of the sentence.

When they had all climbed into the car, Anderson said in a sharp voice, "If I arrested Toney every time he did that, we would have a 100% rise in section 28's. It's a week before welfare day. He doesn't have enough dope in his system to pose a threat. He is just destitute. You should be down here for Mardi Gras at the end of the month, when they all get their disability and welfare cheques."

At that moment, she was interrupted by Lancer. "See, watch this," he said pointing towards the alley. Toney walked out of the alley without the knife in his hands and walked across the street to the pharmacy and went in. He came out a few minutes later with a paper cup in his hands and headed down Main Street.

"His mom lives that way," Anderson added.

Cassidy sat back in her seat and took in the last few moments. She felt ashamed. She felt like she was out of her depth. She soaked it up and never questioned them after that. The two detectives seemed to appreciate that.

"Only a rookie would lock up Toney, and they do, trust me," Lancer said as they turned the corner onto Hastings. "It's a waste of time to treat people that way. They are bad enough as it is."

"Everyone has a weapon down here. We are the least of their worries," Anderson added finally.

Cassidy watched the buildings go by as they drove and thought about the piece she would write. She toyed with different ideas and realized she was actually doing this. Her heart began to fill with purpose, and she exhaled.

3

March 5, 1993

BRIAN OPENED HIS EYES SLOWLY AND STUDIED THE ROOM. HE COULD HEAR the machines around him, and he could see his leg bolstered up with pins sticking out of a very large cast. He could feel the catheter digging in. Brian searched his mind for something he missed, something lost in oblivion. Looking through his mind, he focused gently. The image of his father filled the space, and he began to cry so hard he could hardly breathe. Finally, he caught his breath and wiped his eyes. Anger and hunger came right behind the tears. He pressed the buzzer relentlessly until two nurses came through the door. One had a plate of food and the other a wet towel. She placed the towel over Brian's forehead as he gorged himself on French fries. He fell asleep again shortly after that.

When Brian woke again, it was morning. The light was streaming in through the cracks in the blinds that swayed in the draft created by the machines. He pushed the thoughts of his dad deep within and refused to acknowledge them. He pressed the morphine drip continuously. Every once and a while, the nurse came in and checked something, and then he was left lying there in the stillness again. The doctor came in once a day to talk to Brian about this or that. Then it was back to the silence again. They hadn't been able to get a hold of Brian's mother since the accident. He told them that she worked at the Eldorado Hotel Beer Store in the east end by day and attended bar at Frisco's Hotel in Port Coquitlam at night. She spent the rest of her time with bikers. He never mentioned that.

It wasn't until Brian had been there a month that he was woken in the middle of the night to someone holding his arm and crying. His mother Nicole was there, and he could smell the booze on her. "My baby, what happened to my baby?" she said. Brian looked at her and pressed the morphine drip continuously to stop himself from screaming at her. He pushed all that anger down and just watched her. She had never really been around. When Brian was three, she lost all her hair from stress and threatened to kill Brian. He had been living with his dad ever since.

He looked into his mother's eyes and then looked away. He couldn't talk to her about his dad. He couldn't talk to anybody. She left a short time after that when the nurse came in to check on Brian. "This is my son. I'll come here whenever I want, cunt," was how Nicole decided to say goodbye. Brian had seen much worse on his weekend visits with her. He closed his eyes after that and fell asleep.

4

CASSIDY FINISHED TYPING UP HER REPORT, AND THEN SHE SCANNED IT three times for typos. It had to be perfect. This was her first assignment. She stood up and took a deep breath. She then straightened her clothing, turned, and headed into her boss' office. He was sitting behind his desk with the door open reading copy.

"Hello, Brad. I have that piece you wanted."

Brad looked up at her and motioned with his hand for her to come towards the desk. He took the piece from her and leaned back in his chair, scanning it as Cassidy stood awkwardly and watched. He looked up at her and exhaled. "We can't print this," he said as he threw it down on his desk and leaned forward.

"Why?" Cassidy responded in shock.

"A man was brandishing a knife at 9:30 in the morning, and the cops let him go? Nobody will buy that these cops operate that way. I got a dozen stories where people have been shot for less. C'mon," Brad said, leaning back in his chair and picking his copy back up.

"So, what then?" Cassidy asked in defeated tone.

"You will go with them next week and report something we can print," Brad said, looking over his copy again.

"Next week?" Cassidy asked.

"Yeah, they have scheduled weekly ride-alongs with us to give them some transparency over all these shootings they have been involved in. Those two that you were with have been involved in the deaths of three people in the last year, so don't sell me the 'cop with the heart of gold' bullshit," Brad said, motioning her to leave the office.

Cassidy went back to her desk and threw her article in the garbage. She packed up her stuff shortly after and went home. She was done for the day.

5

ANDERSON AND LANCER STOOD AT ATTENTION IN STAFF SERGEANT WADE'S office. "We have scheduled weekly tours for you and the journalist," he said. Anderson looked over at Lancer as his head went back to absorb the command.

"Why? I thought it was just a one off," Anderson interjected.

"The mayor's office is trying to drown me over the recent shootings and the kid that just died in custody. The Section 28's need to be corroborated with the press; let them see what we are up against. This is redemption for you two, anyways. The last three people you put down are all I hear about in my briefings. What the fuck were you two thinking?" Wade yelled.

"Sarge, you know those were clean shootings. We were cleared," Lancer returned.

"You weren't cleared by the public. That's what this is. Now get out," Wade finished.

Anderson and Lancer put their heads down and walked out of the building without saying a word. It wasn't until they got in the car and were driving before Anderson said, "They will never let this go."

Lancer sped along the highway and never said a word.

6

BRIAN LAY IN THAT BED FOR THREE MONTHS. THEY HAD A FUNERAL FOR his dad over in Victoria without him, probably because his dad's side of the family hated Brian's mother and were afraid she would go to it. Brian started to explore St. Paul's in his wheelchair. He liked the smoking lounge the best because it was located on a rooftop where you could see the whole city. He would go there and smoke with the patrons of the hospital. Sometimes, the staff would chat with him, and other times the long-term patients. Families would also gather out there on the weekend and visit with dear old dad.

Brian missed his dad tremendously. He kept having flashbacks from that day, and his leg would scream in pain when he did. He was given a new drug for his anxiety called OxyContin, and it calmed him down, but he became dependent on it quickly, and his arms started to itch all the time without the drug.

It would be a long time before Brian would be able to walk without the use of a wheelchair, so he was transferred to a place by the Ministry of Children and Families. He was transferred to a group home with a wheelchair ramp. He spent the next couple of years there going back and forth from St. Paul's. The group home was full of boys who transitioned in and out of juvenile hall. Any money Brian had was quickly stolen or taken, so he found a way to hide everything, especially his medication that he relied on on heavily to think straight.

Oxy was a gift if you rubbed off the time-release coating, crushed it up, and snorted it. Brian learned about this when he saw one of his foster brothers doing it with his. The other kids stayed away from Brian,

The Opiate Murders 3

but his wheelchair made him a target for abuse. It was all Brian could do to try to be invisible. Those years taught Brian something he would never forget: Nobody can feel your feelings but you, and nobody will ever be able to truly understand them. Brian learned to keep to himself and not ask too many questions. If he drew attention to himself, he was singled out for abuse by his foster parent, who seemed more interested in cashing his cheque and going to bingo all day.

Sometimes Brian would look for his mother or his Aunt Macey, the dancer – and not the ballet kind either. Sometimes he would find Macey camped out on the Downtown Eastside. She would stay with different people for short periods of time. She was always partying with someone, and she was always happy to see her favorite nephew. Sometimes he went to his mother's work because that way, he knew she would be somewhat sober. The Eldorado Beer Store wasn't far from his group home, so he would cruise up and down Nanaimo Street whenever he needed money. Physiotherapy was hard, but because he was so young, he started to see gains.

On Brian's eighteenth birthday, he aged out of the foster care system. He had full use of a cane now but would never be able to walk properly without one. He was told they would find him a place, and he would receive disability payments every month. Macey knew of a place where Brian could stay, so Brian moved there. It was a place off East Cordova that rented rooms by the month. It had an elevator that worked sometimes, so Brian moved to the second floor.

Macey often stayed with different people throughout the building during the day, and she went out all night. It was always a party when she came home in the morning. One morning, Macey brought Brian in to meet a "friend". Macey rushed around the room, arranging different things as Brian sat down on a chair in the corner of the room. On the back of the bathroom door was a cowboy hat and a long oilskin jacket. Brian studied the jacket curiously and thought about how cool it looked. A few moments later, a large man, who was at least six foot two, came out of the bathroom wearing cowboy boots and wrangler jeans. His façade was completed by a large, white, button-down shirt. His long hair was slicked back, and he had a thick Southern accent.

"Hello, Brian," he said as he reached down and snatched Brian's hand and gave it a shake. Brian's neck went all the way back to take in the sheer size of this man. "I'm Tex," he said finally studying Macey as she fluttered around the room aimlessly.

"Hi," Brian responded.

"I hear you need a job," Tex said after a pause.

Brian was confused for a moment and then he said, "I guess…"

Just then, Macey interrupted. "Yeah, he needs a job. He can't just sit around all day and collect disability the rest of his life." She sat by the window finally and lit a smoke.

"It's a pretty simple job. You don't really need to leave the building to do it, and the better you get at it, the more responsibility you get. How's that sound?" Tex asked, rubbing his side and looking around the room.

"Sure," Brian said.

Tex reached into his jacket by the door and pulled out two bags wrapped in plastic: One was regular white, and the other was black. "Don't mix up these two bags. When someone phones you on this phone, you come down to the lobby and hand one of the packages from one of these bags off," he said, dropping a cell phone in Brian's lap.

"Nobody is to know where these bags are in your place. Got it?" Tex said forcefully. "If I can make you feel one way, I can make you feel the other. Don't fuck with me," Tex warned, looking at Macey and winking.

Macey smiled and exhaled smoke out the window.

"Okay," Brian said, trying to be as convincing as possible.

"When you get the call, it will be either Johnny White calling or Johnny Black. Everything said in the conversation doesn't mean shit except the color. Meet the person in the lobby and give them that color. Got it?" Tex repeated emphatically.

Brian nodded in agreement as the two bags were given to him. He went back to his room with his first cell phone in his pocket. It made him feel important to be doing things for Tex. He immediately saw him as a leader, and he tried to emulate everything he represented. He never looked in the bags, and he hid them well in his place. He kept the phone charged and never used it for anything but business. Brian met people frequently at all hours of the day and handed them Johnny White. He never met Johnny Black.

Months went by with frequent hand-offs. Brian was given money in envelopes that were slid under his door. He saved his money and gave it to his aunt whenever she needed it. He could see she was getting worse. She didn't dance anymore. She would only stay out for days with different fellas. His mother would come by once in a while and degrade him for living there and all the people who lived in his building. She would leave frequently by screaming that everyone who lived there were losers. She fit right in there, but she didn't know that. She wasn't the only person who screamed in the hallways. Brian saved up his money and never deviated from the instructions left by Tex.

One night, Brian heard a knock on the door. When he opened it, it was Tex and Macey. "C'mon, we are going celebrating," Tex said as Macey reached in the door and pulled on Brian's shirt.

"Grab the black bag," Tex ordered as he walked down the hall.

Brian dug out the black bag from behind the toilet and limped down the hall with his cane as fast as he could. When Brian got outside, there was a big truck waiting. Macey helped Brian up into the truck, and Tex patted Brian's shoulder as he got in. The three drove up the street and got onto the highway.

"Where are we going?" Brian asked.

"To a rave," Macey said putting her hands up in the air and screaming as loud as she could out the window, "Yea-haaaw."

They pulled off the highway and on to a secluded road with barely any lights. Finally, they stopped and pulled into a dark driveway. Brian could hear the music and see a structure with lights fighting their way out down the way. Cars were parked everywhere, in every direction.

"C'mon," Tex said, climbing out of the truck.

Macey helped Brian out and started dancing with him towards the complex. Brian's eyes grew wide as he entered a huge barn with lights everywhere, and people dancing on tables and bars. Tex put his arm around Brian and nearly carried him through the crowd. Macey gave Brian a pill and bottle of water she had in her purse, and the three stood there in awe of the sight. There had to be a thousand people there. The DJ up at the front was suspended from the ceiling on a catwalk of some sort, and the speakers on the ground went up twenty feet on each side.

The three of them danced and got high. Brian started feeling the effects quickly. His pain and his limp seemed to disappear by the minute. He had confidence. He had grace. He danced contently and let the music wash over him. Women seemed to pass through him as they came out of nowhere to dance amongst him and his people. The smell of their hair and the shape of their bodies stayed with him long after they had gone.

Tex leaned down towards Brian and yelled in his ear to be heard over the music. "Give me the black bag."

Brian complied and watched Tex part the crowd as he headed towards the back. He could see him talking with some people behind the DJ setup. Brian just continued dancing and lost track of Macey in the process. A beautiful girl came towards Brian through the crowd. She put her hand on his shoulder, and the two of them embraced. She was the most beautiful girl that Brian had ever seen. She had long blonde hair and emerald eyes. Her body was as soft as silk, and she seemed to move around him with such reverence. He never wanted that moment to end.

"What's your name?" Brian asked suddenly.

She looked him up and down and waved her finger at him, shaking her head. She turned around and backed into him, putting all that hair on his shoulder. Brian looked up at the DJ as she slid her body down the front of his and exhaled. She turned around once she came back up and put her lips to his ear and said, "Amber." Then she disappeared into the crowd.

He felt the distance immediately. She was gone. Just then, Tex patted him on the back and motioned for Brian to come with him. They found a lounge behind the DJ where there was a bar and everything. The two sat down.

"I need you to start doing some cutting for me," Tex said, taking a drink from a short glass.

"Cutting what?" Brian returned.

Tex rolled his eyes upwards and adjusted his cowboy hat. "I got a girl coming over to your place this week. She will show you," Tex said, taking another large drink from his glass.

Just then Macey came carrying three drinks for them. "How ya feeling kid?" Macey asked Brian, holding his face in her hands.

"Magnificent," Brian said, and they all laughed. He took another pill, and they all talked late into the night, dancing periodically. Tex disappeared mysteriously from time to time, and then returned, but Brian never saw Amber again. Brian was breathing deeply and sweating buckets it seemed. He started to get cold back in the lounge, so he made his way back to the dancefloor. Soon afterwards, the sun started to come up, and Brian made his way to the door with Macey under his arm.

Tex was standing and talking to two men by the door as Brian and Macey headed towards them. "Brian, this is Willy and David. They own this place," Tex said, introducing them.

Brian looked at them in wide-eyed admiration and said, "This place is awesome!"

The two men laughed and said, "Come back anytime."

Macey hugged the two men as they made their way out the door. The sun blinded the three of them as they made their way out to the truck. As Brian climbed inside the truck, he thought he heard a scream. "Did you hear that?" Brian asked.

Tex looked back at him and said, "Nope."

The three of them drove off down the road, and Brian forgot what he heard. He spent the next day dreaming about Amber and his first rave. He couldn't hold that moment close enough as he drifted in and out of sleep with his legs feeling like they had played a hundred soccer games.

7

CASSIDY SAT ON THE STEPS OF THE POLICE DEPARTMENT ON CAMBIE AND West 5th Avenue, nursing a coffee and trying not to attract attention. She recognized the car as it pulled up and stood up to meet it. She walked slowly towards it, straightening out her bag and clothes. She climbed in the backseat and was quickly met with a couple of rehearsed "Good Mornings." Cassidy sat back in her seat, took a deep breath, and then exhaled in defeat. She wanted to tell the two what her editor had said, but she was too disillusioned to speak. She watched the corners go by one after another, without end, until they parked the car somewhere off Carrall Street.

"We're just going to idle a bit, show our presence, and finish our coffees," Anderson reported back to Cassidy.

Cassidy nodded in compliance as she thought of some questions. Finally, she settled on one from the previous day. "So, last time I was here, I asked you guys about the rise in deaths connected to this new drug fentanyl?"

Lancer looked to his left and tracked someone with his eyes. Anderson put her hand on his forearm and said, "Joseph," Lancer slowly brought his focus back into the situation.

"We have had a rise in overdose deaths involving the synthetic," Lancer said. "It's a hundred times more potent than heroin, and it seems like it only takes a grain of it to put you down" he finished.

"Jesus," Cassidy said writing that down. "Do you guys know where it is coming from?" Cassidy followed up immediately.

"The US has been using it for quite some time along with OxyContin as pain medication. It was only a matter of time before it made its way here," Anderson answered.

"What happens now?" Cassidy followed.

"Well, the counteracting agent is Narcan, so we are using that in our ambulances and hospitals. If the person is found in time, they live," Anderson answered.

"And if they don't?" Cassidy asked quickly.

"They die," Lancer answered.

Cassidy sat back and absorbed the conversation, and looked out the window. "Are you seeing a decrease in overdoses now that you have the reversing agent?" Cassidy asked.

"No, they are on the rise everywhere," Anderson said, sipping the rest of her coffee.

Cassidy took a deep breath and pondered her next question. If she got it right, they might give her enough for a real story. If she got it wrong, they might never talk to her again. She waited a minute or so and then asked, "Can you guys tell me anything about the shootings you were involved in this year?"

Lancer looked out the window and exhaled. Anderson scanned the front windshield for a moment and then said, "Those cases were taken beyond any possible de-escalation. They ended fatally, and we regret the conclusion, but that's the job." Anderson returned.

Cassidy jotted down a few lines on her notepad. "You say you regret the outcome. Can you go into a little more detail about that?" Cassidy followed.

"There was a wave of angel dust that swept the city. The suspects were beyond approach. One of them withstood a taser. Not one – both," Anderson finished.

Cassidy quickly thought about the video of Robert Dziekanski being tasered at the Vancouver Airport and the charges that ensued against the Vancouver RCMP for excessive force. "So, you are saying the suspect attacked you after he was tasered? And then he was shot?" Cassidy asked.

"Yes," Anderson answered.

"How come we didn't find out?" Cassidy followed quickly as she shuffled through her notes.

"Because you don't report on our side of it," Lancer interjected.

Cassidy sat back and thought about the incident. She couldn't believe it. She thought about her assignment and wondered why she was doing it. Why was she sent to talk to these two for her first assignment? It didn't seem like an opportunity; it felt like a cover for something else. "Is there a report somewhere?" Cassidy asked.

"You have access, the official coroner's report, pathology, all that," Anderson answered, annoyed.

"I'll check that out," Cassidy said.

"Thanks," Anderson replied.

Cassidy was swimming in her thoughts after that. So many possibilities.

8

ON WEDNESDAY, BRIAN HEARD A KNOCK ON HIS DOOR. WHEN HE OPENED the door, he couldn't believe his eyes. It was the girl from the night before: Amber. He stood there looking her up and down. Her blonde hair glimmered in the dim hallway lights.

"Aren't you going to invite me in?" she said with a smile.

"Yeah, of course," Brian said, suddenly embarrassed for the mess in his apartment. "What are you doing here?" Brian asked as he closed the door and walked towards the kitchen without using his cane.

"Tex sent me to teach you how to cut," she said with a devious smile.

Brian couldn't believe it. He just leaned against the cupboards and watched her. She was wearing cut-off jean shorts and a black top. Her skin looked so soft and tanned. Brian's place felt bland with its yellow walls and his white skin.

She took bags of product out of her purse and put them on the counter. "We'll start with the white package," she said, as she looked around the kitchen. She cleared the countertop and dumped out a large bag of whitish-yellow powder. Brian had never seen that much dope in his life. Not even in the movies. She then took out a large bottle of OxyContin and a yellow box.

"Hey, I have those pills here," Brian said pointing at the OxyContin.

"I use it to buff the base, and then we add caffeine. Keeps 'em coming back steady. That Oxy is super addictive. We once ran out of the H, so we crushed up and served it with some caffeine and creatine. They couldn't tell the difference."

Brian watched her work. She crushed up the Oxy using a small sifter that she had with her. Then she mixed it in with the larger amount of heroin that was spread out on the tabletop then she sprinkled in the caffeine. She used two playing cards to sift the dope with. They were aces of spades. Brian watched her knead the dope over and over and over, until all the colors were one. She took a deep breath away from the counter and lit a smoke.

"Now we bag it," she said. She took a deep drag off of her cigarette and looked at Brian leaning against the cupboard with his eyes transfixed on her. He could tell she liked the attention. She started bagging the mix into large bags with white paper inside. "Never mix the two batches, and always use white paper inside the angel package. Angel white, you see?" Amber said to him.

Brian watched her scrape the tabletop clean. She then gave the package to Brian. "Now stash this somewhere," she commanded. When Brian had come back from the bathroom, she was crushing an altogether different substance in her sifter. They were yellow pills, and she wore gloves and a mask. She sifted it down into a yellow powder and spread it out on the countertop. Then she added caffeine, sifting it as she did before, and bagging it up without a word.

"What's that?" Brian asked.

Amber looked up at him and said, "This is the black package – fentanyl. It is smaller and goes into tiny black dime bags." She sifted carefully, making up the bags as she went. Brian was sweating from watching her. The air was full of dope and tension. When she finished, she handed Brian the bag and said, "Don't get these two mixed up. Hide it in a different place entirely."

Brian nodded and followed instructions. When he got back, Amber was running her lighter underneath a spoon. Brian looked her up and down and said, "What now?"

"We test it," she said with a smile. "Always test the white; never touch the black," she said emphatically.

Brian nodded and took a couple deep breaths. Amber took his arm and wrapped a small rubber band around it. She looked it up and down and said, "Virgin arms. The vein just floats on the surface." She took a needle from her purse and sucked up the substance in the spoon through a small piece of filter into the syringe, stopped and looked Brian in the eyes. She leaned forward and he met her halfway. The kiss seemed to last forever. Brian's whole body started to heat up.

The two parted lips, and then she inserted the needle into his arm. He felt a deep ache and then a wave of euphoria rushed through his veins. He leaned back to catch himself. He was led towards his bed and then he was lying down. The ceiling became a myriad of colors in a cool, clear expanse. He sweated through his clothes, and his mouth was moist with the taste of adrenalin. Amber did her own shot beside him on the bed and then lay down.

The two held hands on that soft bed in that dingy yellow apartment somewhere down off Cordova, but to them, they might as well have been in the grandest palace, with woven tapestries that cascaded down from fifty-foot ceilings. The breeze coming through the window from the Downtown Eastside became the cold whisper of the River Jordan or some remote spot in the Indus valley.

Brian was overcome with rapture for this new life. He drifted in and out of consciousness with her there. They smoked, they laughed, Brian threw up in the bathroom. It was the greatest afternoon of his life. He embraced his new beginning and left his dad and the accident behind him.

9

WHEN CASSIDY ENTERED HER EDITOR'S OFFICE, SHE WAS CAUGHT OFF guard. "I thought I told you I wanted something I could print!" he said to her as she tried to sit down. "No, don't sit," he said annoyed as he shuffled through pieces of paper on his desk. "Do you understand our business, Cassidy?" he asked dismissively.

"Our business?" Cassidy answered.

"Yeah, what we do here, and how we do it?" he said as he looked right at her and stood up straight.

She could feel the whole office watching her from behind the glass. She felt very small. She swallowed hard and said, "to inform our readers of the truth?" she said rhetorically. "It is to seize their attention and give them our take on the world. Do you know how we do that?" he asked forcefully.

"No" she answered as she looked down and then raised her head slowly so she could at least see his desk.

"Internet is 80% of our revenue, people out there with phones who don't know what a newspaper is. We grab their attention with thumbnails. Do you think that exonerating two police for three 'good shootings' in one article is going to do that?"

"Yeah, but I have the pathology report. It was PCP that sent those suspects overboard. One of them stabbed two people and robbed another before he attacked them after withstanding two tasers. This guy was out of his mind," she said catching her breath.

"You see, right there. You say Mental Illness, not PCP. You say information is being withheld. You leave the reader with an impression that they should not trust the police and trust us. You need them coming back to us to check if everything is okay. You know, I thought because you were young, pretty, and naïve that they would open up to you. Give us a good story. But you can't even do that." He shook his head as Cassidy studied her shoes.

"Get out of here. You go out one more time next week, and if you don't bring me something I can print, you're back on personal assistant duty permanently. Now shut the door."

Cassidy kept her head down as she traveled through the office and down the stairs. She opened the door to the back alley as she held back a river of tears. She exploded as soon as she felt the air on her face. The raw grip of emotion was so heavy in her stomach she almost threw up. She struggled to find her smokes and light one. She exhaled as her hands shook. She rocked back and forth thinking of anything else she could until the feelings subsided. She was afraid to go back inside, she didn't know where she belonged anymore if it wasn't inside. All she ever wanted to do was be a reporter, like Lois Lane or Diane Sawyer. The real world was far too cold to her right now. She would find a place she could feel safe and start fresh tomorrow.

10

WHEN BRIAN WOKE FROM HIS DREAM, HE WAS MET WITH THOSE EMERALD green, eyes of Ambers staring at him. He thought it might have all been a dream. She lay there completely naked, with one leg over him. He ran his hand down her thigh and rested his hand on the back of her hip.

"Good morning," she said deviously. The two became one; awkwardly at first, but they found the rhythm that came to them so fluidly when they were high. The morning sun beat in the window as they threw every ounce of energy at each other. Brian went to the kitchen quickly after to get some water. He didn't use his cane. He gulped a glass of water down quickly and then filled the glass and brought it to her. He watched her drink and found it hard to focus on the scene.

Was this really happening he thought. He looked at Amber finally and asked, "How do you know Tex?" he asked skeptically.

"He's a friend of my dad's. Tex used to drive truck up north," she said offhandedly as she pulled the covers over top of her and rested her head on the pillow, watching him.

"How long have you been cutting?" he asked curiously.

"As long as I can remember," she said, without a care in the world it seemed. "I used to ride with my dad sometimes. There are lots of stops on the road. We sold dope to other truckers."

"And now you are here," Brian said.

"Yes, I am," she said with a smile.

"Do you want some coffee?" Brian asked.

"I would love some," she said as she turned her face into the pillow and yawned.

The sun cascaded over her body, creating a halo. Brian stood in that doorway one more moment to take it all in, then he set himself to the task at hand. They went out for breakfast after that, Amber told Brian about her world. She was an art student. She painted and sculpted. She danced in an off-Broadway show. Brian felt very far from home when he listened to her talk. She introduced him to this whole world behind things that he didn't know was there.

Amber went home sometime after that. They kissed in the street and said their goodbyes. "I'll come see you soon," she said.

"When?" he asked.

"That's the fun part. You never know."

He watched her walk towards the SkyTrain and disappear in the crowd. He exhaled deeply as he turned around and headed back to his life. His life felt so devoid suddenly, like he was missing his shadow. He went home and slept the day away, thinking of her draped across the bed in the morning sun. All that blonde hair and those emerald-green eyes shining in the sun.

11

CASSIDY CLIMBED INTO THE CRUISER ON WEDNESDAY MORNING READY TO work. She had used the last few days to improvise a plan.

"Good morning," Anderson said to her as she settled in her seat.

"Hi, good morning," Cassidy replied.

As they drove through the streets, Cassidy became quiet. She listened to the police scanner go off a few times, breaking the silence. She thought about her job and how much she always wanted to be a reporter and took a deep breath. What came out next was a step towards journalistic integrity, but a step away from her job.

"What do you think about reporters?" Cassidy said randomly.

The two in the front seat started to laugh. They didn't answer, but they laughed pretty hard. "Thanks for that," Lancer said as he made a left turn onto Carrall street.

"Do you guys think you are represented fairly?" Cassidy followed.

"I would say, 'No comment.'" Anderson replied with a laugh.

Cassidy quickly changed up her strategy, if that's what you call it. "My boss wants to bury you guys. He won't print anything I write. I thought I wanted to be a reporter, I'm not sure anymore," Cassidy finished.

The car pulled over to the side of the road, and the two officers got out and left Cassidy in the car. She could see them arguing. Lancer's back was turned to her, and Anderson was walking out in front of him. Cassidy expected the worst.

How could she be so stupid and unprofessional, she thought. She had crossed the line, and she knew it. The bottom of her stomach dropped out as she awaited the judgement that was coming for her.

When the two officers got in the car, Cassidy put her head down and thought of an apology. "Guys, I've had a rough couple of weeks. I didn't mean…" Cassidy was saying as she was cut off by Anderson.

"We were ordered to drive you around by our Captain because they want us to play into your boss' hands. They want us to take the fall for the way the system is set up." Anderson said.

Cassidy was blown away by the comment. "How do you mean?" Cassidy asked quickly.

"The mental health calls we get are a dirty bomb. We show up, and the person is suffering from mental illness, substance abuse, sleep deprivation – you name it. They are usually male and heavily armed with weapons due to paranoid delusions, and we are sent there to intervene. The situation happens dozens of times a week. The system creates these situations because there is no preventative supports in place, and those people become delusional psychopaths because of it. The damage is done long before we ever arrive, and a lot of the time, the person is killed by us because it's set up that way. I was trained to be police. Police protect and serve the law. The law states, if you assault innocent people for any reason, you are a threat that needs to be neutralized immediately. Nobody wants my job because I have to make a snap judgement – life for others or death for this sick individual right now. You reporters feed off the violence that is perpetuated by this system, we clean it up," Anderson finished.

Cassidy felt an overwhelming urge to fix the situation. "What can we do?" she asked.

After a few moments, she got her reply. "We will show you what is really going on, and in return, we would like something from you," Anderson said.

"Anything," Cassidy returned.

"We would like you to go public with what you find. We don't care who with; it just has to happen," Anderson replied.

"Okay," Cassidy said, sliding back from her leaning position that she didn't realize she was in. "My boss needs me to write a piece about you guys that you won't like," Cassidy said.

"We don't care, as long as we are solid on the first thing," Anderson returned.

"We are," Cassidy said in a voice that she was proud of, a voice she could believe in. She had taken her power back, and from now on, she would be her own broker.

12

BRIAN WOKE UP TO A KNOCK ON THE DOOR. WHEN HE GOT UP AND answered it, he found Tex standing ominously in the doorway.

"Morning," Tex said as Brian backed up to let him in. "I heard you met Amber," Tex said looking around the room.

"Yeah, she's great," Brian said, thinking back to the weekend.

"I need you to come with me right now. I have some business to attend to," Tex said.

"Okay," Brian said without a moment's thought.

"Grab, two out of the black bag," Tex commanded.

Brian found the black bag and grabbed two bags out of it and got dressed. He followed Tex for a couple of blocks and around a few corners and through an alleyway. Before Brian knew it, they were standing in front of a rundown hotel. Brian followed Tex in and up two flights of stairs. Brian's leg was getting better; he barely noticed the flights and he didn't really use his cane.

Tex banged on a door, and the two waited there. The door opened after a few minutes, and Tex was led inside by a man that looked like he just woke up. "What's up today, Leroy?" Tex said loudly with familiarity.

"You know, not much. I meant to call you yesterday, but I was busy with my sister in New West," Leroy said scratching his arm and looking Brian up and down.

"This is my associate Brian. What's your middle name, Brian?"

"Daxon," Brian returned quickly.

"Dax is my associate," Tex corrected himself.

"Hi," Leroy said with a bow. Leroy's place was small with garbage all over the place. There was a chair by the window and a bed on the floor; the rest was bike parts and debris.

"Here, have a taste, I have a job for you to do," Tex said, motioning for Brian to give him one of the bags.

Brian searched in his pockets and gave Leroy one of the bags. Leroy snatched at it greedily and headed into the kitchen and rummaged through the cupboards. Leroy shuffled past the two of them and sat down in the chair by the window. He quickly started dumping the contents of the package into a spoon and then lighting the bottom of it with a lighter, while he sniffed and jerked left and right in the chair.

Tex lit a cigarette and offered one to Brian. Brian lit a smoke and took in the aroma that was now filling the room. He was transported back to the weekend with Amber. His mind wandered to that place with her as he looked out the window that began to fill with smoke as it barreled out the window. Brian watched Leroy ready a shot with a needle sucking up the contents of the spoon with it. He tied his arm off quickly as Tex stood in the kitchen, leaning against the counter staring at the roof. Leroy steadied the needle between his fingers looking for a vein on his pale, white arm with the tourniquet clenched between his teeth and wrapped around the top of his bicep. When he was done, he pulled the needle out and placed it on the windowsill, rubbing his arm after.

He tilted his head back and said, "What do you need me to do?" as he exhaled.

Tex turned and watched Leroy's head tilt all the way back. It wasn't until a couple minutes later that Brain could see the blue in his lips and a white complexion wash over Leroy's face.

"Die," Tex said in a cold voice.

Brian's eyes shot from Leroy's face to Tex's. Leroy let out a huge gargle that scared Brian, and he stepped back beside Tex.

"If you have a problem with this, that second bag is for you," Tex said without even looking at Brian as they watched Leroy's last moments.

Brian followed Tex out, and he shut the door behind him. When they both emerged on to the street, Tex turned to him and said, "If you ever say anything about this, remember it's your fingerprints on that bag up there." Then Tex kept strolling down the block. Brian didn't know what to say, so he didn't say anything.

"'Dax' that has a nice ring to it. We are going to have a wonderful apocalypse together. Welcome to the Union," Tex said, and then he walked away leaving Brian there.

Brian headed straight home, looking over his shoulder constantly to make sure he wasn't being followed. When he got home, he paced back and forth. He thought every siren he heard was coming for him. As the days passed, he realized nobody was coming. He set into a routine of dropping packages off all over the Downtown Eastside. Sometimes white and sometimes black. He answered whenever the phone rang and did what he was told. He never spoke to Amber about what happened. He kept the darkness deep inside.

13

THE TITLE OF THE ARTICLE STATED: "COPS DODGE THE RAP ON THREE Shootings in the Downtown Eastside." Cassidy could see her boss' head nodding up and down from her little cubicle across the office. He never asked to see her, and the story went up on the site immediately. It got fifty thousand views in the first fifteen minutes it was there.

Cassidy felt for a moment that feeling all journalists feel when they produce something everyone wants to read. It was addicting. She kept checking the page and the comments. People were pissed off. They ranted and raved in the comments section. There were 276 comments in fifteen minutes too. Some as simple as "bring back street justice" to "fuck the police."

It was clear the city didn't trust these cops, and Cassidy could see why. They were always portrayed this way. Like they had done something wrong, and nothing was being done. Cassidy thought about the executioners they had become for a system that liked to chew people down to the base and then throw away the core.

In the meantime, she was busy working on her story; silently, gently, putting the pieces together. She couldn't wait till next Wednesday.

14

BRIAN WOULD DO SOME DROPS AT PLACES HE HAD NEVER BEEN BEFORE – hotels that weren't hotels, and businesses that weren't businesses. He was careful with his fingerprints now; he always made sure to handle bags without leaving any. Brian was walking back to his place one morning when he was stopped by two squad cars. They came up fast on him, and a number of officers jumped out. He was pushed into an alley and surrounded.

"Good morning, you must be the new bag man," one of the officers said as he punched Brian in the stomach, and another kicked him in the head when he hit the ground. Brian was dizzy and couldn't see who was hitting him.

"I guess you are the new Leroy, now that he's dead," another cop said over the muffled sounds Brian could hear while he lay in a covered position.

The last thing Brian felt was one of the officers stomping on his hip and breaking his cane. He lay in the alley for a long time after that. He thought he was going to die. When he woke, he was in the hospital again. Amber was holding his hand.

"You're going to be alright, you just can't walk for a while."

Brian was relieved. "What did the man say?" he asked.

"He says you are getting a new place to live and to hang in there," Amber said with a smile, running her fingers through Brian's hair.

Brian couldn't imagine what he had done in this life to deserve this angel of a woman, but he accepted her care gratefully. In the days to come, his mother would be escorted out of the hospital multiple times. Macey even came to see him, which was a relief as she had been missing in action. He started physical therapy and got back on his feet slowly. He leaned heavily on his new cane, and he could feel the plate in his hip piercing his bones and tearing at his flesh. He would lay in his bed sometimes and pray for the end. *How could a life be filled with so much pain?* he thought. He would close his eyes just like he did the first time he learned about his accident and wish he never woke up. He always did, but it didn't hurt to ask.

15

THREE MONTHS LATER, BRIAN WAS RELEASED FROM THE HOSPITAL AND brought to his new home. It was on the top floor, and it had an elevator. He could see Gastown from his balcony. Amber walked him around and showed him all his amenities. "Do we take care of our own or what?" Amber said triumphantly.

Brian was excited, but he quickly found a bed and lay down. Amber pulled a bag out of her purse and set up a shot for him. As he felt the pin prick his vein, he was transported to the place beyond right and wrong, to a place beyond pain and expectation. He sweated through the sheets and came in and out of states of consciousness. Amber fixed and lay beside him; they fell asleep holding hands.

When Brian woke there was a knock on the door. It took him a long time to get there. When he finally opened the door, Tex was standing ominously in the doorway again.

"I heard you were back," he said as he stepped around Brian and walked inside. Brian closed the door slowly and limped inside, leaning heavily on his cane. "I'm sorry for the other day, and what happened to you after that. Some people are born into this, and others are chosen. I would say you were born into this thing. I took you there to show you what becomes of men when they pass over the line. Let me ask you something: How often do you need to re-cut and bag up?"

Brian thought about it for a second, like he was reaching back. "A couple times a week, maybe more," he answered.

"Would you say the demand is larger than the supply?" Tex asked.

"Definitely," Brian answered, realizing that he wasn't in danger. He sat down at his large table and lit a smoke.

"You know what that means?" Tex asked him, while staring out the window.

"No," Brian said staring at Tex intently.

"It means that we need to thin the herd. You see this dope game is like any jungle. You have your apex predators roaming the top: cops, doctors, psychiatrists, and then us. The pyramid is supported by all those citizens out there. Some of them take a drink, some smoke, and some poke. The doctors and psychiatrists sell their product, the cops take their cut, and we drag the rest," Tex said, lighting a smoke.

Brian didn't know what to say. He had never thought about it like they were all working together.

"You see, Dax, you have to make a decision. Do you want to hold your place at the top, or do you want to descend to the bottom? I can't always protect you, but I can always piece you back together," Tex said, stepping out on to the balcony and flicking his smoke off it.

Brian thought for a few moments and answered, "I'm with you, man."

Tex stared at Brian for a moment and then said, "I'm glad you said that. I never doubted it." He reached into his pocket and pulled out a new cell phone and a large stack of money. "For your pain. We'll keep in touch," he said as he strolled out of the apartment and closed the door.

Brian exhaled when the door shut. He stared long and hard at the money and the phone. A part of him was excited, but a part of him was terrified. He felt so weak and ineffectual since the assault. He thought about his future and what was to become of him as he stared out at that foggy city with its abdomen exposed. You could literally see the jungle from his perch; the wasteland began at Water Street and extended east as far as he could see. He knew his place in the world at last – another east-end parasite taking that last drag off a person's soul and putting them out in the ashtray of Pain and Wastings.

16

WEDNESDAY MORNING CAME, AND CASSIDY WAS POISED TO GET TO WORK. She waited on those steps with excitement and vigor. When the car pulled up, she moved towards it gracefully and climbed in the back seat. The three of them drove down to Main and Hastings and parked the car.

Anderson was the first to say anything, and she wasted no time. "Are you familiar with this area?" she asked Cassidy.

"Yes, sort of," Cassidy returned.

"Before Riverview even closed, we began to see what the future was to look like. All of these pharmacies started to have lines coming out of them. The patients that were released from Riverview were given homes, that's true, but before they closed permanently, they stopped taking in patients that were critical or in their first years and just kept long-term patients. They played the stats because they knew they could track long-term patients better and receive the results they wanted. We started seeing the results of this thinking immediately. We started seeing an influx of people residing in SRO's – that's single-room occupancy – in the community. These were people without addiction problems who were sick from a range of different identifiers. Whoever accepted them down here is the type of addict they became. If the alcoholics accepted them, then they became alcoholics. The junkies, then they were using heroin. Crackheads, well now they were smoking crack, the list goes on. What was already a threat to their own safety was now being exacerbated by other substances.

"These new people would become heavily sedated on whatever these doctors were giving them, and then they would be mixing other substances. Some would start to steal to feed their habits and others would sell their bodies. Do you know how long a wait it is to get into housing supports down here for the mentally ill now that Riverview has closed?"

"No," Cassidy returned.

"At least a year," Anderson replied. "And I know of people that are still on the list after two. Our job down here is to enforce the law and engage this population respectfully. We get 30% of our calls, 150 a day, for people down here. When we show up to deal with the same people over and over and over, it gets tight, like you saw with Toney the other day. Other times, the person is nonresponsive, delusional, suicidal, and homicidal.

"We have to put them down in some capacity, and there is nowhere to take them. We lock them in city cells until they stabilize, and then we send them back out to do it again and again. What's the record?" Anderson asked Lancer.

"I don't know," he replied.

"Joseph…" she repeated

"My mother called me Joseph," he said.

"Well?" Anderson repeated.

"Fourteen incarcerations in a week for Bill Akerman," Lancer exclaimed.

"How's that work?" Cassidy asked.

"We let them go at 6:00 a.m. and have them back in sometimes by 6:45 a.m. They go right to the Tim Hortons across from the SkyTrain station and cause a scene," Lancer explained.

Anderson continued the thread. "So, what I said to you the other day happens every day, but we don't always know the person and sometimes people get hurt, and the patient turns into a suspect. That is how people get killed. We are not equipped to fight this war. The politicians, doctors, and psychiatrists condemn these people to these conditions, and we mop them up."

Cassidy leaned back in her seat and thought about what had been said to her. Then she said, "You forgot to say then the news makes it look like it's police brutality."

Anderson nodded her head in agreement. "They blame us for everything, but it started long before we ever came into contact with these people," she replied.

"Where should I start?" Cassidy asked.

"Right there," Lancer said pointing to the medical clinic.

Cassidy looked over and asked, "Why?"

"Think of it like this: The doctor puts you on six different kinds of meds, knowing you will be down here for at least a year, without money for food or proper care. Then you see over there?" Lancer asked.

"Yeah," Cassidy said.

"That's Insite. They have the safe injection site over there. You are in a wind tunnel here. One side of the street gives you drugs, and the other side gives you drugs, what's the difference? The end result is the patient being strung out and desperate. They either kill themselves or get into a situation where we have to engage them. We don't always know what to do with a homicidal maniac. They weren't one when they got here. They were just a person who needed help. This is the system, and we are sick of taking the blame for it. That's what we want you to write," Lancer finished.

"We are going to give you the addresses of some people who just got here. We want you to see for yourself," Anderson added.

"Great," Cassidy said.

"Here are two addresses. One's a young man who just arrived, and one's a woman both are in their early 20's. *Both* are from the Greater Vancouver area," Anderson said shaking her head.

"What?" Cassidy questioned the sarcasm

"Well, if we don't have you follow people from Vancouver, the powers that be will 'other' the findings," Anderson said.

"*Other* the findings?" Cassidy asked.

"They will say that they were a problem case that was sent here from another province and dismiss the treatment of that person outright," Lancer finished.

"Wow," Cassidy said, shocked.

"They blame immigrants for everything, even if they are our own Canadian citizens. All you have to be is from somewhere else not to matter," Anderson said, shaking her head.

"I got it," Cassidy said, taking the addresses.

17

ONCE BRIAN'S LEG GOT BETTER, AMBER AND TEX TOOK HIM TO THE FARM for a rave. He was excited to do something that wasn't cutting dope. It's all he seemed to do these days. When he got in the truck, Amber rubbed his shoulders from behind him, and Tex shook his hand. They arrived at 1:30 a.m., and the place was hopping; everywhere he looked, people were dancing and getting high. The bar was swamped, but Tex just walked around back to get drinks.

"Come dance with me," Amber said pulling Brian into the crowd of people.

She put a pill in his mouth and turned around rubbing her body against him as he downed the pill. The room got brighter, louder, and more intense. Brian couldn't move as well, but he leaned on her when he had to. He had learned early on that dancing with a girl is all about her; you just had to sit back and watch the magic happen. Amber loved to dance, and she was captivating to watch. Brian just stared at her and looked into those deep green eyes.

After a while, Brian had to sit down. He found a place next to Tex and some people. He took a drink from Tex and downed it. Amber downed hers too.

"You want to see something?" Tex said to Brian.

"Sure," Brian responded, feeling very high all of a sudden.

Tex motioned to Amber to stay there, and led Brian into the back behind the bar and DJ. He led him down a hallway and opened a door. When the door opened, there was a large room with purses and shoes covering the floor and a door to a huge pig pen at the far end. The lights were halogen and immediately hurt Brian's eyes. Tex closed that door, crossed the hallway to the other side, and opened another door. Inside that room it was darker, and he could see people on couches having sex. Some were smoking crack, and some were injecting heroin. Brian followed Tex into that room and took it all in.

Tex motioned to two girls sitting together to come over. "This is Brian," Tex said to them.

"Hi Brian," they both said in unison.

"Take care of him, will ya?" Tex said with a laugh.

The girls took Brian back to the couch they were on and took Brian's pants off. Then they both took turns giving him a blowjob until Brian was ready for anything. He took one at a time riding him while the other kissed him. He looked around him as he did it and could see multiple couples doing the same. He never came that hard in his life. The girls continued kissing each other after they were done with him.

Brian stood up and pulled his pants up. In that instant, he saw Amber across the room. She was naked with a woman between her legs staring at him. She was moaning and pulling at her hair. Brian took a few steps forward to make sure it was her. She winked at him, and Brian froze there captivated by the sight. She motioned for him to come over, and he came and sat down beside them. Amber grabbed at his arm as she climaxed.

He lit a smoke. As he exhaled, he watched a man carry a woman on his shoulder out of the room. He put his head back and closed his eyes. The girls sat on either side of him and rested their heads on his chest. He didn't want the moment to end. The sun came up shortly after that, and the three drove back to the city without a word; the music said everything.

18

WHEN CASSIDY STUDIED THE ADDRESSES THAT ANDERSON GAVE HER, A cold chill ran up her spine. Even in a job where she mostly got coffee and ran errands for the first three years, the buildings she was to visit were infamous. The Balmoral and the Regent. Timothy Walters in the Balmoral was her first visit. When she arrived outside, she met the eyes of the vagrants outside. They were curious about her. They couldn't place her. She wasn't a cop, maybe a social worker, but they stared long and hard at her.

When the door opened, she was hit by the hot breeze that came out of the building, a mixture of mold and cigarette smoke. She made her way through the hallways looking for the room. Some doors had number's others it was in black felt marker; some not at all. There was black mold on the ceilings, and it looked like there had been a fire at some point. The smell got worse, the higher she went. She had to cover her mouth to breath.

Finally, Cassidy reached the door and knocked on it. There was no answer. She was about to give up when she heard a voice. "Who the fuck is that?"

She stopped and listened before replying. The door opened a crack, and she saw a young man with no shirt on and messy hair staring at her.

"Are you Timothy Walters?" Cassidy asked as forcefully as she could. She didn't know if she should be there. She felt that nobody should.

"Who's asking?" he said, looking her up and down.

"I'm a reporter hoping to get your story on the conditions down here since you arrived," Cassidy said as officially as she could. He looked her up and down again dismissively. "I brought cigarettes," she said, finally reverting to the plan that Anderson had mentioned. *They won't want to talk, but they will smoke cigarettes*, echoed in Cassidy's head.

"Let me see," he said forcefully.

She showed him a brand-new pack of Player's Light, and he quickly opened the door. When he opened the door, Cassidy wished she hadn't asked. The room was so small that Cassidy's arm span was almost the width. The walls and ceiling were black with mold. It looked like there had been a fire that never got cleaned up. There was a bed on the floor – a thin mattress with a sheet on it. A lawn chair with a milk crate in front of it sat in front of an open window with burned spoons on the ledge. Used needle packages littered the floor. To her left, sat a shelf built into the wall, lined with bottles of pills in all shapes and colors.

She took a deep breath and handed him the cigarettes. He disappeared to the right where there was a sink and a fridge and lit one of the cigarettes. The smell of the cigarette made the room smell better, and Cassidy searched for her nerve to question this man. She found it somewhere around her thought of leaving. "How long have you been here?" she asked finally after much internal debate.

"Since December," he said.

It's July now, so seven months, she thought. "Are you on a waiting list for housing?"

"Yes."

"How long have you been on that?"

"Nine months. I was on the street before this," he said sniffling and taking long drags off his smoke.

He was skinny; he couldn't have been eating much. His eyes were blue but dim, and they kept darting around the room and back to her. He finally sat down in his chair and put his feet up on the crate in front of him.

Cassidy relaxed and eased into her real question. "Do you mind telling me what designation you are classified under and what meds you are on? I want to give our readers the sense of urgency you are under to secure permanent psychiatric housing," she said hesitantly

"Are you fucking out of your mind? You're not printing anything like that. Who sent you?" He quickly stood up and came towards her. She started to panic. He got within inches of her face, and she could smell the sweat and anxiety on him. "Well!?" he screamed at her.

"I'm just a reporter. I am writing a piece about the conditions down here and what it takes to secure long-term housing in the Downtown Eastside," was all she could say.

Her hands were shaking, and he could tell that he was scaring her. It was all he needed. He backed off quietly, but never stopped staring at her. She pulled out her cigarettes and lit one. He nodded at her gently, and she caught her composure.

"It takes a lot of suffering to get one of these rooms, and you are nearly dead by the time you get into permanent psych housing," he said finally after a long pause.

She didn't know what to say now. She studied his surroundings. The fridge door was open, and it didn't appear to work. The floor was stained and dirty. The only window was cracked slightly and covered with a sheet that swayed with the wind behind it.

"Thank you for your time," Cassidy said, excusing herself and closing the door behind her.

She passed people in the hall and kept her head down. She heard screams in the distance, but she didn't turn to hear where they were coming from. By the time she came out the front door, she was gasping for breath. She had almost passed out from the heat inside.

She got the point. Anderson wanted her to see the conditions of the people that they usually reported as junkies, crazy, and criminal. They looked more like conditioned, medicated, and desperate to her, and maybe that was the point. Conditions create a population, not the other way around. It was neglect, greed, and indifference that led a slum lord to profit from that place.

Cassidy went home instead of going to the second address. She couldn't do that again today. Tomorrow or the next day maybe; she didn't know. She couldn't get the smell out of her reality, or those walls, those floors. There were stories that bodies are buried in those walls, and she believed it. The smell confirmed it. It was low-income housing, built on the bones of dead prostitutes and junkies, and subsidized by the government for the mentally ill. She could never write that, but some realities we never speak of because they are too true to accept.

19

BRIAN WOKE ONE MORNING TO A BANG ON THE DOOR. HE KNEW THE sound. When he opened the door, Tex walked in agitated. "You seen Macey?" he asked accusingly.

"Not since I was in the hospital. What happened?" Brian asked.

"She's been going around fronting dope on my name. She's done it everywhere. If she doesn't straighten this out, she's going to the farm," he said furiously.

Brian was scared for her and himself. After Tex left, Brian made his way down to the Eldorado to ask his mom where Macey was. When Brian got there, it was before noon, so he got to see his mom sober – well, as sober as Nicole could be. She always had a drink in the morning to steady the hands, and then she would take a handful of ephedrine to speed up the rest.

When Brian came to the door, she was sorting out empties with a customer. They laughed a bit, and Nicole handed the customer her receipt and the money. "Say hi to your dad for me," she said with a tone reserved for movie stars. Brian barely recognized her. He always marveled at her beauty and poise. There wasn't a place his mother would go that she wasn't admired. But then, she would start to drink around 4:00 p.m., and all that loveliness drained from her and was replaced by malice, deceit, and cruelty. Brian shook his head at the thought of it.

Just then, Nicole saw him. "Oh, Janice, this is my son, Brian. Isn't he handsome?"

The woman stood back and said, "yes he is, Hi Brian," she said as she left the store.

"What's up?" Nicole asked, looking at Brian's cane and studying how he walked.

"Can we talk outside?" Brian asked.

"Sure. I'm just going out for a smoke," she yelled at the office behind the counter where a very small man sat in a very small space.

When they got outside, Brian went into it. "You seen Macey?"

"No," Nicole said, lighting a smoke.

"Well, she fucked up. People are looking for her."

"What people? Those fuckin bottom feeders can get in line. She already owes money," Nicole said, exhaling and fixing her hair in the window.

Brian stood back and leaned on his cane. These women didn't give a fuck about anything or anyone. They weren't afraid of anything. "Well, if you see her, Tex came around looking for her. Tell her that," Brian said.

"Tell, that mongoloid to fuck off, Brian. He could never do anything to her, trust me," Nicole said, flicking her smoke out into traffic. "Now, I gotta go. Take care of yourself," she said as she hugged Brian and headed back in.

Brian made his way back to his place, in his way, stopping every couple of blocks to rest his leg. He cursed the fates and downed more Oxy. He needed the pills for everything now. He could feel the metal grinding his flesh and bone. He never realized that pain could bore holes in the brain, but that is what it felt like before he took his pills.

He would shoot with Amber when the time was right, and they could just be alone. His life had become very isolated because of his injuries. When he got back to his place, he looked out over the east end and hoped Macey was hiding out somewhere nice. Maybe she started dating a nice biker, or she could be the top girl for an old pimp. Maybe she went back to dancing, and that's where she was, dancing on a circuit. Brian pushed his fear aside as he settled into his couch. The pills took him off to sleep, down past the street and all its villains, down past all his physical ailments into that field. He stood in a golden field surrounded by wheat blowing in a gentle breeze. He closed his eyes and opened his arms to it; he welcomed it. Death.

20

CASSIDY STOOD OUTSIDE THE REGENT HOTEL, ONE OF THE MOST NOTORIous addresses in the Downtown Eastside, conveniently one block from the Balmoral. She stared down at the piece of paper in her hand, and then looked forward. She took a deep breath before going in. The lobby was hot, and it was all Cassidy could do to not take deep breaths. The building smelt like cigarettes and moldy beer. She made her way up to the third floor, walked down a hallway, and slowly approached the door for which she was looking. After straightening herself out, she knocked on the door.

"Who is it?" was all she heard.

"I'm looking for Jena Rollings," Cassidy said intently.

A man opened the door, and she could see a woman sitting on the bed before the man closed the door behind him and came within inches of Cassidy's face. "It's twenty for anyone to go in there," he said to her. His breath was disgusting; she had to turn her head to avoid it.

Cassidy looked at him puzzled. "I'm just here to ask her some questions," Cassidy said reassuringly.

"Listen, whatever you want costs twenty, just like everyone else," he said looking her up and down.

Cassidy finally took two steps back and reached into her purse and rummaged around. She was sure not to show her wallet, as she cleverly fished out the only twenty, she had and gave it to him.

He opened the door and said, "You got thirty minutes."

Cassidy entered and stood awkwardly in front of a bed as the door closed behind her. Cassidy looked around the room but only saw caps of needles and burned spoons on the window ledge. She looked to the counter in the kitchen and saw pill bottles and pills strewn across it.

"You got a smoke?" Jena said breaking the silence.

Cassidy complied and lit one of her own. The two avoided eye contact and smoked their cigarettes.

"How long have you lived here?" Cassidy asked out of habit.

"Four months," Jena said quietly.

"Where were you before that?" Cassidy followed.

"I'm from Chilliwack," she said, wiping her blonde hair from her eyes.

Cassidy could see that the makeup Jena wore was covering up a bruise on her jawline. She sat with a blanket around her waist. She was wearing a halter top, and her skin looked grainy and dehydrated.

Family there?" Cassidy asked, hoping she might persuade her to go back.

"Can't go back," was all Jena said.

"How long have you been seeing the doctor?" Cassidy asked.

"Since before I came here," Jena said quietly.

"What is your designation, if you don't mind me asking?" Cassidy asked.

"I'm bipolar with a touch of schizophrenia," she said with a smile.

Cassidy smiled back at her and asked, "what pills are all those over there?"

to which Jena looked over and said, "wake up, mid day, go to sleep."

"You use other substances too?" Cassidy asked quickly.

Jena nodded. In that moment, there was a bang on the door. "Hurry the fuck up," the man yelled.

Cassidy started to take panic breaths, her eyes darted left to right thinking of a question, none came to mind.

"Thank you for your time," was all Cassidy could say. She handed Jena a pack of smokes, which Jena quickly hid under the blanket, and then Cassidy opened the door.

"Don't come back," was all she heard as she walked down the hallway. When she got outside, she started to walk down the street, choking back the tears. She stepped off into an alley, went down on one knee, and started to cry.

Just then, Cassidy heard the sound of a cart and a man humming a tune: "Sweet Caroline, oh-oh-oh." She wiped her face and stood up slowly taking in the sight of him. He was a little taller than her wearing a baseball cap with his black hair tied back in a ponytail. He had on sandals with jean shorts and an unbuttoned khaki shirt that showed his dark skin with numerous necklaces with feathers in them. He pushed a cart lined with dream catchers. He didn't have empty bottles in it, but rather he had bottles of water, white T-shirts, socks, and other things of that nature.

"Are you a social worker, dear?" he asked with a resounding voice that resonated comfort and concern.

She sniffled and continued to wipe her face. "No," she answered.

"We get at least one social worker a week out here crying," he said reassuringly.

"I bet," Cassidy said, collecting herself and lighting a smoke.

"Yeah, they come down here with that caring degree, and they burn out like a comet," he said equivocally.

"How's that?" Cassidy asked.

"Well, a lot of these people that are sent down here have never been here before. They have it in their mind that they are going to change the place. Like it's not supposed to be like this," he said.

Cassidy took a long drag off her smoke and bit down hard on the comment. "You think it's supposed to be like this down here?" she returned.

"The world is a mess, and it's always been a mess. It's not your job to save it or change it. Your job is to get right with yourself and the Creator. If you do that, the rest will fall into place," he said to her softly.

"I don't get that," Cassidy said.

"All these people are trying to fix their own lives through helping and changing things in the external world, but the world only appears this way because they are trying to do that" he said, offering her a bottle of water. She took it thankfully.

"My name is Clark," he said extending his hand to her.

"I'm Cassidy," she said with a nod.

When he began to move his cart along, she scratched her head in disbelief that she suddenly felt better and yelled out after him, "Do you mind if I walk with you a bit?" to which

he replied, "Sure, c'mon."

The farther they got away from the building, the better she felt. "Where are you from?" she asked him

"Right here. I was taken from my village by the government when I was six years old and put in the residential school. I've been down here since I'm sixteen years old," he said confidently

"I'm sorry to hear that," Cassidy said dropping her eyes to the ground.

"A lot of my people that went to those schools never came back, so I'm grateful to the Creator for my life and my days out here," he said as he pushed his cart, stopping to talk to people in alleys under cardboard boxes. He handed them water, clean socks, and T-shirts. He treated them with respect and dignity, and then he moved on.

Cassidy followed him like a lost puppy dog not knowing what to do or where to go next, so she just followed. He had a way about him that she didn't expect to see down there. Everything that she knew about Hastings was bad, especially after her last two interviews. He changed that for her, she didn't see the people down there as equals. She felt sorry for them, ashamed even, but Clark acted like one of them. He moved his cart slowly but confidently through the streets, and people came out from every crack in the wall to hug him. It was like being with a celebrity. He was like the medicine man of Hastings Street. She had completely forgotten about the incident at the Regent and moved slowly and confidently with him up and down the block.

She left Clark a short time after that with a dream catcher in one hand and a white T-shirt in the other. She sailed back to her place on the winds of change. Her perspective had changed. She looked squarely at the carnage of people's lives and just saw the life. She looked to her own life with confidence and gratitude. Gratitude for her little apartment, her job, shoes on her feet, food in her fridge. She found peace in the last place she would ever look for it – inside herself.

21

ON A BRIGHT, BEAUTIFUL THURSDAY MORNING, WHILE EARLY MORNING cyclists and commuters made their way to work, Macey was found dead in a staircase off Cordova. No press or bystanders were there to greet the body as it was rolled out on a stretcher and fed into the back of a dark blue Econoline van with no windows. Two taps on the back door from the cop who escorted the body, and the van rolled away.

The news of her death travelled fast. Brian knew within an hour, but Nicole knew right away. Brian went to his mother's work to see her, but she wasn't there. He headed down to Carrall Street next for answers. When he got to Tex's, he stopped for a moment and caught his breath. He was frantic. He banged on the entrance to the building, and a tiny slit opened at eye height, and a voice said, "Whatchew need?"

"The Man," is all Brian said. He stood out front and waited for Tex. Fifteen minutes and two smokes later, Tex came out, struggling to pull his coat over his shoulders. He looked forward at Brian, who stood to meet him.

"What's up?" he said, adjusting his hat and pulling a smoke from his ensemble.

"Did you hear?" Brian asked forcefully, not knowing what would happen next.

"Yeah," Tex said, letting a barrel of smoke leave his mouth and trail down the street.

"What the fuck?" Brian said next forcefully.

"Listen kid, we didn't do this. If we had, we definitely wouldn't have left her down there in some staircase. You know we send them off to the farm. Plus, Macey was worth way more to me alive than dead. She was a smooth operator when she was on. She fell in with the wrong people. She didn't care who she was using with or when, shooting her mouth off about this or that, and she got done. That story will play itself out down here till kingdom come. You know that" Tex said, extinguishing his smoke with his boot. "You wanna go for breakfast?" he asked.

The two of them made their way up to a breakfast joint and sat down. They ordered, and Tex continued on. "She will be sorely missed, Brian."

Brian sat there and drank his coffee in a daze. He couldn't stop thinking of his mother, even though her and Macey hadn't spoken, and if they did, they would have instantly been fighting. His mother was going to go off the deep end about this. The oldest of the sisters had already committed suicide when Brian was seven. It was something they never spoke of but was ever present in the substance abuse of the two remaining sisters. They both used to infinitum, Macey with the drugs, and Nicole mostly with the booze.

"My mom isn't going to make it," Brian said finally, staring Tex in the eyes.

He nodded, "It's going to be close."

Brian couldn't eat anything when the food came. He just sat there and watched the people in the restaurant eat. His world had stopped but the rest of the world seemed to just go on without him.

22

NICOLE NEVER WENT BACK TO WORK, AND BRIAN NEVER SAW HER ALIVE again. She was found at her apartment in Port Coquitlam. She had downed a bottle of sleeping pills with a bottle of vodka. Brian's nervous system shut down at the news. He couldn't get out of bed. Amber would come and fix him with heroin to ease the pain, but it just added to the numbness. Somewhere down deep in his psyche he would have conversations with himself. "What is the point?" would be the theme of any and all correspondence and the answer would be "There isn't."

Time just seemed to drag at that level, on and on across fields of time. He would watch the water run down stream in his mind until it reached a vast ocean of emptiness. He looked upon the ocean and marveled at its endlessness. He imagined a better place beyond the street and the hotels. Beyond the pharmacies and safe injection sites. Across the water, there was a shore; he imagined them all over there.

He imagined the three of them sun tanning and drinking margaritas, their brown skin shining in the sun. He envisioned a better place for all of those lost souls down there on the corner of Pain and Wasting's. He longed to bring them release. He longed to end his own suffering through the ending of theirs. He saw his predicament as an opportunity instead of a tragedy. He would become that which he most feared: death itself. He would apprentice himself to Tex in every capacity he could find from now on. It was the only way to take his power back.

23

WHEN CASSIDY GOT INTO THE CRUISER ON WEDNESDAY MORNING, SHE felt like a different person. As they drove through the streets, she saw the terrain with different eyes. She saw what Anderson and Lancer did from their perspective, the city was set up like a game of chance. If you were lucky enough to never ask for psychiatric help, kept your head down, and worked, you were able to avoid the abyss. But if you weren't, it was all the way down you go.

She could see naturally that it would start with the doctors. They were looking to pick up some of this big pharma money that psychiatry had unleashed. They would give you a script for pretty much anything after an eight-minute interview. Most of the clinics were walk-ins, so there was no follow-up or psychiatrist involved. The doctor just prescribed and spun the wheel.

The closing of Riverview had flooded the market with fresh prospects descending on the Downtown Eastside along with evictions from all over the lower mainland. The question was: Who can afford to take a year off work to handle a psychiatric illness? Would disability pay a mortgage? The answer was an overwhelming 'No!'

So, people ended up down here, and who do they meet when they get down here? The doctor first, then maybe a five-minute psych appointment, but they can't afford anything more than that. Then they end up living in these ghettos down here, submerged in rodent, and bug infestations like rats, scabies, and lice. From there, people assimilated into the drug culture, giving whatever they have to get high every day and self-medicating with pills until they have a violent episode and get shot by the police in a total psychotic delusional state. They get bagged and tagged, and somebody comes and takes their place.

Cassidy sat there and didn't say a word. "I'm guessing you checked them addresses?" Anderson asked.

All Cassidy did was look at her and nod resolutely.

"You can see why we need your help then?"

Cassidy nodded again. She thought for a second and then said, "I'll need another angle to throw you guys under the bus with, just to keep the wolves away while I investigate" Cassidy explained.

Lancer looked out the window and said, "Well, there's always the pay increase we are fighting for right now in the union. You could mention how the people on welfare are living in squalor while we go back to the bargaining table to get more money for a job we barely do."

Anderson laughed stroking his arm and saying "Joseph, you could have been a reporter."

They both laughed, and Cassidy cut in saying, "It's actually pretty close." They all laughed.

24

THE NEXT TIME BRIAN MET UP WITH TEX, IT WAS A BLOCK FROM CARNEGIE Library. Tex was standing on a stoop overlooking Main and Hastings. "Good morning," Tex said, motioning for Brian to sit down beside him.

"I've come to ask you to put me on," Brian admitted.

Tex took a long drag from his cigarette and said, "I thought you would never ask."

When Brian sat down, Tex began to talk. "Now, in order for you to do this job, you have to understand a few things. First of all, you have to understand how we are able to do this without being caught. You can't kill anything fresh, and what I mean by that is this: The public perception of people down here is that they chose this life. A young person down here dead doesn't look like they chose it; they look like a fucking victim, for Christ, sake.

"We wait. Everyone loves these young girls who come down here from everywhere and start hooking, life is good. They are like a fresh piece of fruit, but then everyone takes a bite, and then we throw out the core. You understand? Nobody is going to miss an old, washed-up whore, but a young girl who made a few mistakes is a victim. She will be on the news. Don't get me wrong. Sometimes people come looking for the missing person, but the public doesn't care about them, so we are good. Understand?

"You send them to the farm if you snatch one. You call Cookie, and he'll send the van." Brian nodded.

The Opiate Murders 3

"Men are fair game. Get what you can as far as muscle is concerned, but all in all, nobody ever really cares when a man dies, so we are good there."

Brian nodded again. Tex stood up, and Brian did too. Tex looked out over Main and Hastings and looked Brian in the eyes. "What do you see?"

Brian answered, "Death."

Tex pointed to the intersection and asked, "What do you see?"

Brian answered, "Opportunity."

Tex patted Brian on the back and said, "If you do well, you will become one of us; one of the Union front runners."

Brian's eyes grew wide at the prospect of becoming. Purpose waits for us all; in that way, Brian had found his.

The kid was a natural; nobody could deny it. In his first month, he dropped five bodies: two out in the open and three went to the farm. He had a talent for enticing people through his injury and his youth. He sat and waited. He didn't rush. He had time. Brian observed the rules: No young women. Let them have their time, but once they timed out, these men would take them. Brian watched like a lion in the jungle, learning to hunt.

Sometimes he would lose out because the woman would disappear, but all in all, he was getting to know the schedule of the hookers down there. He knew who the pimps were and who was vulnerable. He would see Amber once and a while, but he would always be distracted. They would use and sleep together, but it wasn't the same.

One morning, Amber looked at him and said, "My mother used to say that my father made the highway cry he was gone so long on it. I'm starting to feel that way with you. You aren't here with me. You are somewhere else," and she left.

Brian had a taste for death; he couldn't think of anything else. Amber's dad was in the Union. He was a truck driver like Tex, and he had the fever. Brian could taste death in his mouth when he stepped into the street, like a vampire. He would canvass the neighborhood and then he would sit and wait. He had lots of cover; between the ambulances, police, and crime, he looked like a saint. He peddled his dope, helped who he could, and made friends with the locals. He blended right in. Then if that wasn't enough, Tex would walk around with him, and they would talk.

Anyone who saw Brian with Tex would immediately stay out of Brian's way. It was like being under the wing of a dragon. Brian picked up a new trick here and there as he waited to be anointed by the Union. The street was like a farm team; hookers, gangsters, and killers are picked off the top once they make their mark. The rest fall to the wayside. Some in painful ways, and others just waste away into compost, giving rise to the next budding star.

25

CASSIDY SAT AT HER DESK, WATCHING HER EDITOR READ HER COPY. THE byline read: "Fresh Off Their Shooting Spree, Veteran Cops Seek Higher Pay." *He must be salivating,* she thought as she headed out of the office for the day.

As she made her way down Granville Street, she stopped at a bar to have a drink. It was Thursday, and that meant only one thing to her – relaxation. She ordered a drink and sat at her regular table. Her friends would be there eventually, she thought. They all had jobs that required locked-in schedules that mostly ended at 4:30 p.m. If she had her copy in, she could do as she pleased. She loved journalism for that.

As she sipped her drink, she met eyes with a man across the bar from her. He stared at her for a second and then said something to the waiter. A moment later, a large margarita with an umbrella in it showed up at her table. It nearly took up the whole thing. She scoffed as the drink was set in front of her. "From the gentlemen at the bar" was all the waiter said as he stepped away with a smile.

She looked over at the man, and he had a huge smile on his face. She laughed and said to herself, "He better come over here and help me with this drink. Who does he think I am?"

In a moment, he finished his drink, stood up, and headed towards her table. He was tall, with sandy brown hair. Cassidy figured he must work in the financial sector because he had on those shiny black shoes that bankers and start-up CEO's wear. He was wearing loose-fit blue jeans and a black, long sleeve shirt. He worked out – lots. It was apparent.

"What's your name?" he asked without sitting down

"Cassidy," she replied with a smirk.

He had green eyes. *They suit him,* she thought.

"Can I sit?" he asked.

"If you can fit in with me and my drink," she replied.

"I'm Derek," he said extending his hand and shaking hers lightly as he sat down. "What are doing in a place like this?" he said quickly.

"Just having a quiet drink and waiting for some friends," she said, sipping her original drink.

"I thought you looked like you needed a vacation; that's why I ordered it," he said, nodding at the tropical monstrosity.

"Does it show?" Cassidy said, staring at him sideways.

"Not from where I'm sitting, he said staring into her eyes. She quickly looked away after a moment. "What do you do?" he asked.

"I'm a journalist," she said. For the first time, like it was for real. She had now published two articles – crime articles, not puff pieces about bake offs or blood hounds – but about real crime.

"That's interesting. What kind of journalist?" he asked, leaning forward.

"Crime right now. I'm doing stories about the Downtown Eastside," she answered.

"I work in securities. I can see it all from my office," he laughed.

She smiled. She thought about how those two worlds were right beside each other. In a lot of places, the homeless population and the day traders share a street corner. Junkies & Junkies people would say, the only difference is how they dress. She laughed to herself.

He knew he had lost her. "My dad was a cop in New West, and my mom was always scared for him when I was growing up. I didn't want to do that to her again," Derek said, sparking her interest.

"That must have been taxing. I ride with a couple cops every week, they seem exhausted," she added.

"Yeah, my dad couldn't wait for his vacation time. He never talked about his work," Derek said, motioning the waiter to bring him a drink. "Should we get you a regular drink?" Derek asked.

"I thought you were going to help me with this one," she teased.

"Well, we are on vacation," he said with a laugh, taking one of the straws and taking a sip. "That is sweet," he said, watching her drink from the other straw. They both laughed.

Just then, Cassidy's friend Amanda came in and waved at Cassidy. Cassidy waved at her, and Derek stood up. "Well, it was nice to meet you. Can I have your number? I thought we could go on a real date," he said.

She reached in her purse, pulled out her note pad, and wrote her number and her name on it. "Just in case you forget it," she said handing it to him. Amanda looked on, as if she wasn't paying attention.

"I'd never forget it. Bye," is all he said as he took the number and walked away.

Amanda strolled up a moment later and said, "Oh my God, he was cute. How do you know him?"

"We met on vacation," Cassidy said with a smile.

"Some vacation," Amanda said, raising her eyebrow and watching him walk out into the street.

26

IT HAD FELT LIKE A LONG TIME SINCE AMBER HAD HEARD FROM BRIAN when he called and told her he was coming over to her house. He had only been there once in all the years they had known each other. When Brian got into the elevator, he could taste death in his mouth. He had killed three women that week. He reached into his pocket and pulled out a double shot of Narcan in a syringe and injected it into his leg. He took a deep breath and then put the syringe back into his pocket. When he stepped off the elevator, he caned his way to the door and knocked gently.

That beautiful face brimming with excitement came to meet him at the door. "Hello" was all he said as he stepped inside and sat down on the couch. He took a glass pipe and filled a piece of tinfoil with dope and ran a lighter underneath. He inhaled that yellow nightmare and then handed it to Amber. As he watched her take a hit, the bottom of his stomach fell out from fear. He watched her absorb the dope and then put her head back, she instantly reached for his leg as she went down. He lay there with her until he heard her gag and gargle for breath. She was the last hold out between the worlds for him; the only thing keeping him here. He watched her take her last shrieking breath, her face turning white and her lips blue.

"I want you to come with me, darling. I can't die without you," is all he said as he watched her fade away. As her body grew cold and her spirit left, he slid the pipe from her hand and put it into his pocket. He would carry her wherever he went now, until it was time to join her.

But she would never be alone. She would always have company. *Dax would make sure of that,* he thought.

He closed her eyes, put a blanket over her, and left the front door open as he left. As he walked down the street, he thought every ambulance was coming for her. He came alive when that feeling rushed through his veins. This world was cold and hard all the way through. He would save his victims from that. He would help them to the other side. This life had too much pain in it to be beautiful to him anymore. All he saw was death.

27

TEX CAME STRAIGHT TO DAX'S APARTMENT TO CONFRONT HIM WHEN Amber was found dead in her apartment by a neighbor. "Did you hear about that?" he yelled at Dax when he came in.

Dax looked him up and down from the kitchen and said, "Why would I kill her? She is worth more to me alive than dead. I loved her for Christ sake." Dax answered as he lit a smoke and showed no remorse.

Tex stood at the door and marveled at what he saw. Brian was gone. Dax had taken his place. Tex had killed Macey he would never admit it though. He saw that same look now mirrored back to him. Both men looked at each other from across the apartment and saw the same thing: death. Tex knew Dax's time had come.

"We'll be in touch," Tex said as he shut the door. Dax stood there for a moment and thought of all that had transpired in the years leading up to that moment. He had been chosen; he could see that, a man forged in pain and anguish to become an instrument of deception. He would take the pain away. He would take everything up in a cloud of smoke. He limped over to the window and envied his victims. Dax longed to be with them, but not yet. His romance with death had just begun.

28

CASSIDY WALKED INTO A MEDICAL CLINIC ON MAIN AND FILLED OUT A FEW forms while she waited for the doctor. "The doctor will see you now," the receptionist said a few moments later. When Cassidy walked through the doors, she was greeted by a nice-looking lady.

"Hi, I'm Doctor Fincher. What can I help you with today?"

Cassidy looked around that little room and sat down on the examination bed. "Well, I recently moved to the neighborhood. I'm waiting on a housing application for assisted living, and I'm really anxious," Cassidy said, scratching at her arm and lowering her eyes.

"Have you been on any kind of anxiety medicine before?" Fincher asked, looking at the chart.

"Yes, but I can't remember what it was," Cassidy said, looking down at the floor.

"Well, I can put you on a sedative and a mild medication for sleep," Fincher said, ticking some boxes and writing down a script. She handed Cassidy the prescription without batting an eyelash.

Cassidy took it and put it in her purse. She wanted to say something so badly, but she was too appalled to blow her cover. She thought about the Regent Hotel, which she had listed as her address, and the young woman she saw there the other day and shook her head. She thought about the counter full of pills beside a fridge that didn't work in that hotel room.

Cassidy left the doctor's after that and stood outside for a moment, gathering herself before the next experiment. The appointment with the doctor to get that prescription had taken eight minutes. She lit a smoke and stared at the safe injection site across the street. She took a long drag off her cigarette and waited for a tug to come from inside her. Her hands began to shake as she crossed the street.

Cassidy walked up to a window and said, "Can I get in there?"

A voice from inside said, "You got any dope?" to which Cassidy said, "No."

"Well, there's no grinding here. You gotta bring your own dope," the voice said.

"Where do I find some?" Cassidy asked.

The person in the window motioned her to the alley next door. "Don't come back without dope. I want to see it in your hand," the voice said.

Cassidy nodded and then walked to the nearest alley. Her heart began to pound as she looked at a couple people sitting on the ground against the building. She heard a whisper from the other side of the alley behind a garbage can. "You lookin'?" Cassidy nodded.

"Gimme twenty," the voice said. Cassidy reached in her purse, pulled out twenty dollars, and handed it over. She was given a small, black, see-through dime bag with a white rock in it.

She quickly marched back to the window and showed the bag to the person inside. She heard a buzzer and the door opened. She was then faced with a waiting area with a few people in it. One person took a long look at her and then banged on the door. "Hurry up, you fuckin' cunts. I ain't got all day."

Cassidy sat down in an empty seat, eyeing the dope she was given. She could feel the eyes on her. Just then, the door opened and the few people waiting were ushered in, leaving her there alone. She looked around at the graffiti on the walls and the debris on the floor and imagined what it was like for people to come here day in and day out. She was scared, but she was very alert as well. She hadn't been that electrified ever.

The door finally opened, and she was faced with a whole room staring at her as she came in. There were twenty booths. All cooking and smoking with the smell of heroin, crystal meth and cocaine. There was a big-screen TV on the wall, playing the news. She felt like she was at an airport.

She looked for the nearest woman and walked up to her. "How do you get out of here?" was all she asked.

"Through there," the woman said, pointing to some doors. Cassidy handed the bag to her and walked out. When Cassidy came out the doors onto the street she was panting. Her teeth were clenched, and she was surrounded by that smell of sulfur. She lit a smoke and walked on down the street.

Just then she heard a familiar voice "Back for some more punishment, are ya?"

Her head swung around to see Clark standing with his cart.

"Hi again," she said blushing.

He nodded to her, looking her up and down. "Coming down to save someone, are ya?" he asked.

"No, no… No saving anyone down here," she returned, remembering their conversation.

"Are you okay?" Clark said, looking at her shaking hands.

"I'll be alright," she returned covering them up inside her jacket.

Clark stared over her shoulder at where she just came from and said, "A lot of people lose their way down here. Some come back, and others don't." He reached inside his pocket and pulled out a bracelet made from shiny black stones. "This is Apache tears. You carry it with you while you are grieving. It will absorb your pain. Bury it somewhere beautiful when you are done," he said with a smile.

Cassidy took it graciously and then hung her head. Clark handed her a bottle of water and went on his way. She stood there watching him chant something as he crossed the street. She thought about the doctor and the injection site. This was a gauntlet. The people forced to live here didn't stand a chance. It had taken longer to get in the safe injection site than it did to get the prescription from the doctor.

29

IN 2002, THE FARM WAS RAIDED BY POLICE AND THE BROTHERS WERE taken into custody, but only one was charged. The farm was exhumed and traces of twenty-seven bodies were found on the premises. Only six murders were charged, and only the one brother was sentenced to twenty-five years in prison. He was originally charged with forty-nine missing women, but the crown decided to narrow the charges to ensure conviction. Tex and Dax left town in the semi-trailer and headed north. The highway connecting the northern communities with Vancouver would be their home. They would sleep in hotels and gather the souls at night that hitchhiked between rest stops.

Prince George was the city that held most of their business and contacts since the raid on the farm. Dax would take weeks off sometimes and stay in a town, concocting different combinations of dope and poisons. He became very astute in chemistry. He read lots about alchemy and how one substance could turn into another with the right mixture and patience. He hoped to create a substance that would take souls quickly and gently. He wanted a seamless poison: fast-acting, potent, and untraceable.

He would meet girls in the local bars and carry on, relationships. Everything was going fine until he was picked up for sleeping with a minor, and his hotel was tossed. Small-town cops put a bell around his neck and sent him to the Regional Correction Centre for statutory rape and drug possession. He spent that time in protective custody reading and trying not to be killed by other inmates. He was there for two years. When he was released, he only wanted to go to one place: the Downtown Eastside.

30

CASSIDY STOOD IN THE LOBBY OF 555 WEST HASTINGS STREET, WAITING for Derek. She was a little early, so she stood outside and had a smoke. She had only taken a few drags when she felt a hand on her shoulder. She turned, and there he was dressed in a suit and tie with his jacket hanging over his forearm and a briefcase in his hand. Derek was the epitome of a Vancouver day trader.

"Are you ready?" he said kindly as he led the way into the building and into the elevator. Once the elevator started going up, the shaft disappeared, and the Vancouver skyline engulfed them. Cassidy stood back in the elevator from the shock of being up that high. She took a deep breath as she watched the city roll out before her in all its magnificence. She smiled at him as she steadied herself by putting one hand on the side of the elevator.

A moment later, they had arrived at the top. Derek led the way into the revolving restaurant and sat down at a table against the edge. Cassidy sat down across from him and took in the view. "I haven't been here for a very long time," she said.

"I was about to say the same thing," he laughed. "It's funny that all these tourists come from all over to see these sights, and I walk by them every day and don't notice," he said with a look of regret.

They both ordered drinks and looked at the menu. He ordered a steak, and she ordered the lamb shank. "So, how's the newspaper business?" Derek asked nonchalantly.

"Well, lately it's been a little less than I imagined," she said taking a long sip of her drink and staring back at him.

"How, so?" he asked.

She sat there for a moment and studied him. Then she asked, "What do you make of all the homeless and drug-addicted people down here? You must see them all the time."

Derek took a sip of his drink and answered, "I think it's tragic, but it seems like a permanent thing down here."

"I've been working around Main and Hastings with two cops lately, doing an exposé on police shootings," she said.

"I read it," he answered with a smile.

"You did?" she replied.

"Yeah, I was sifting through your paper, and there you were," he said.

"I guess we are between the front page and the business section," she returned.

"I thought it was harsh how those cops got away with murder," he responded.

She stopped for a minute and took a deep breath. "It's not really like that," she said, taking a drink and looking out the window.

"How do you mean?" he asked.

"I mean there's a lot more to it than that. We don't report that though," she finished.

He looked out the window and nodded. "If it bleeds, it leads," he said finally.

"Exactly! Whatever we can embellish for the sake of ratings, we do," Cassidy said, relieved that she didn't have to explain further.

"What about you, Wall Street? How are the captains of industry doing?" Cassidy asked.

"Well, you know, it's up and down," he said with a smile.

"like, literally," Cassidy said with a laugh. She felt relaxed with him.

"Where are your parents now?" she asked.

"They moved up to Salmon Arm. They bought a bed and breakfast up there, and my dad does fishing charters," he said.

"No PTSD?" she asked.

"I don't think PTSD was invented when my dad was a cop," he replied, and they both laughed. "You just did your job and tried to make it home alive," he finished.

Just then the food arrived, and the two of them spent the rest of the time eating, you can always tell that the food is good if there is silence during a meal. Towards the end, Derek said, "Thank you for eating. It's such a rare thing to see a girl who is hungry!"

"Well, you probably see a lot of hungry girls just none who are willing to do anything about it," Cassidy said with a devious smile.

He laughed and motioned the waiter for dessert. They shared a piece of chocolate cake with whip cream and chocolate drizzle cascading all over it. "This was fun. We should do it again," he said looking over at her.

"What makes you think this is over?" Cassidy said with a laugh.

When they got in the elevator, he was facing her with his back to the city, and she gave him a look he couldn't ignore. As the weight dropped out from beneath them from the descent, they kissed. Cassidy leaned forward into him and held him till the lift stopped. They stepped out into the street holding hands, but afraid to look at one another.

They found a bar on Georgia, played pool, and got really drunk. He rode with her in a cab to her place and watched her go in. When she woke the next morning, she thought she dreamt the whole thing, but the headache and the hangover reminded her of the reality. She still had her clothes on in bed. She plugged her phone into the charger, and after a couple minutes, she read his text: "Next time we'll do brunch." She smiled. "Certainly" was all she replied.

31

IN 2007, DAX GOT HIS BIG BREAK: FENTANYL HAD COME TO THE DOWNTOWN Eastside. People were dropping like flies from smoking dragons. There was always a fair share of intravenous deaths, but never before was a drug so potent in small doses that nobody was the wiser when someone went down. He started buying kilos from China for a thousand dollars a piece. They spread the work around now that they didn't have the farm to dispose of bodies. Abbotsford and Chilliwack fit the bill. There was always lots of places there to dump bodies. Time just went on like that.

Dax was welcomed into the brotherhood of the Union. Tex had vouched for him, saying: "This young man might not look it, but he's the darkest I've seen." Dax spent all his time creating different variations of poison. Fentanyl was in all of it. By the time the Riverview closed its doors in 2012, Dax and the Union had cleared hundreds of souls in plain sight. Everything was blamed on the toxic drug supply.

32

WHEN CASSIDY GOT IN THE CAR ON WEDNESDAY, SHE WAS READY TO WORK. She immediately followed up on a conversation she tried to have the first day she met Lancer and Anderson. "I have been meaning to talk to you guys about the rise in overdose deaths involving the new synthetic opiate, fentanyl" she asked.

"Fentanyl has been a silent killer in these streets for a long time now. It is only lately that it has been mainstream news," Lancer said, staring out the window at the rainy day that was upon them. The wipers flashed across the windshield, playing with the red and white lights in the excess rain.

"Just like Riverview, this all started a long time ago," Anderson interjected.

"Do you think that some of these deaths are deliberate? I mean, there are just so many," Cassidy asked, quickly gaining momentum.

"Probably," Lancer said.

Anderson looked over at him quickly and snapped, "Officially, it's a sad fact that 80% of the victims we find had someone with them before their death. That person either phoned the ambulance or just walked away because they didn't want to deal with it."

"How often do you find people like that?" Cassidy asked.

"Too much," Lancer finished.

Cassidy sat back for a minute and gathered her thoughts. She thought of all the angles and then she picked one. "Have you guys ever charged anyone for murder?"

The two cops were silent up in the front seat, then Anderson turned right around and said, "We charged a woman named Bloody Mary once. She was found with a half dozen bodies in a three year period," Anderson said.

"But she walked," Lancer finished.

"Why?" Cassidy asked.

"For the same reason she was committed to Riverview, or sorry I should say, was committed to Riverview, who knows where she is now," Anderson explained.

"Why didn't the charges stick?" Cassidy pressed.

"Because she was crazy; she talked about how ghosts and some mysterious 'them' group made her do it," Lancer said.

"What 'them' group?" Cassidy asked.

"You know, *them*," Anderson said, pointing up to the sky.

"Aliens?" Cassidy asked.

"Maybe, or who knows, the CIA, FBI and the list goes on," Anderson said flippantly.

"Six bodies seems like a lot," Cassidy continued.

"Depends, where you are. If you are in White Rock, then yes. If you are down here, no. Those ambulances are running all day and all night for that sort of thing down here. You know how people fly into Las Vegas to gamble? People flock to these streets from all over to die," Lancer said.

"That's just one demographic," Anderson added.

"How many demographics are there?" Cassidy asked.

"Did you go to those addresses I gave you?" Anderson asked.

"Yes," Cassidy answered.

"Well, that's one. There are many other people who come down here. There's the newly released from prison population. There's the recently divorced and lost their job population. There's the aged out of foster care population; survivors of the residential school's population; those who go from being on disability to being on psych meds in the upper-class neighborhoods yesterday, only to be cast down here today; and the list goes on and on. It's a mess," Anderson explained.

"How do you guys make sense of it all?" Cassidy asked finally after a few moments of looking out the window.

"We look at it from a tactical perspective. We assess and prioritize immediate threats and leave the rest to the other sectors, like social workers and the lot," Lancer answered.

"What happens when the other sectors are creating threats?" Cassidy said, thinking about the doctors and the psychiatrists.

"We finalize those threats either through force or confinement. We don't prevent; we are a last resort," Anderson said.

Cassidy thought for a while and then asked, "What's the solution then?"

Anderson took a deep breath and said, "A miracle."

33

SOMEWHERE IN THE EAST END OF VANCOUVER THAT NIGHT, THERE WAS A gathering in the basement of one of the old buildings far out of sight and sound. A large group of men cloaked in black were gathered. At the front of the pack, stood a large man who was also cloaked in black, but white cloth sashes hung from him, almost like a catholic priest. However, this was no religious service. Tonight, the Union was honoring a fallen soldier. Earlier in the week, one of their own had been killed by police.

Dax and Tex stood in the back against the wall, both would glanc around the room and then back at each other. They knew what was coming. The man at the front of the room with the sashes was their leader. He was well known in the group as being one of the founding fathers. He lit two tall torches that stood on either side of the podium and then the lights went dim.

"Brothers, tonight we have gathered to honor one of our fallen angels who died in battle. He was one of the bravest men I've ever known. He stood for something. He had purpose, and tonight we are here to spread that purpose all over this city."

The room started to erupt in shouts and the stomping of feet in unison.

"Tomorrow is a day of reckoning. Tomorrow is a day of grace. Bow your heads with me, brothers. Though he may lay low, he is not deep. Even though he is gone, he is not far. The righteous never die!"

With that, the two torches were extinguished. In the dark of that room was silence; in the dark of that room was purpose. Tomorrow many would die. Red death was distributed to every man, and tomorrow the whole city would feel the grief of the Union.

34

WHEN CASSIDY GOT TO WORK THE NEXT DAY, THERE WAS PANDEMONIUM. The police and ambulance services had been overrun with overdoses since early morning. There were as many as ten deaths before lunch, and it didn't stop all day. By the time Cassidy went home, she knew that sixteen people had died, with hundreds of other overdoses reported across the lower mainland. The experts said it was a toxic supply. The cops believed it to be a phenomenon of epic proportions, starting downtown but then spreading as far as Mission. The papers reported the families of the victims and ran stories about law and order. In one corner of the city there was solace; in one corner of the city there was relief. In the depths of Carrall Street, the men of the Union rested easy.

35

CASSIDY'S RIDE-ALONG WAS POSTPONED FOR A COUPLE WEEKS, WHICH left her with a lot of free time on her hands. She decided to take some initiative and cross-reference police shootings with waiting lists for mental health housing. There were ten shootings that year, and eight of those people had either been on the waiting list or had been previously released from some form of mental health housing. The other two couldn't be more different. The other two couldn't be more sinister.

Larry Crawford shot last week in a standoff with police. He had numerous sexual assault charges going back to his teens, unlawful confinement, aggravated assault, and assault with a weapon you name it. He was shot by police after being pulled over, he opened fire during a routine traffic stop injuring one officer before being shot himself and dying at the scene. In the trunk of his car, they found three women bound for transport for what the report called "human trafficking".

"What the fuck? How come we didn't get this?" Cassidy said to herself staring down at the papers. *This was just last week,* she thought. She was about to phone her boss when she looked at the other death. She shuddered and lost her breath as she focused on it and the date. Last spring, a man named Lester Carnal was killed by police after a chase that started with him being caught having sex with the corpse of a woman in a hallway of an abandoned building. Police responded to an anonymous tip of a woman being assaulted at that address. When the police arrived, they chased him out the back of the building and shot him in the alley.

The Opiate Murders 3

Three days later, there was ten overdose deaths in the east end. It was deemed the worst "Mardi Gras" of the year in the paper. It occurred on welfare day: one of the heaviest times for overdose deaths in the month. More people overdose and die in the three days before and after welfare day than all other days of the month combined. Carnal had a long list of sexual assaults. Had been in and out of prison his whole life.

When Cassidy looked at the two instances, she didn't need it to connect; she knew it did. In all that randomness, there was a pattern; in all that disgusting randomness, there was a thread. She pulled addresses for these two men, and the story got more and more clear. Both men had worked as truck drivers earlier in their lives. Both men had done time in the same places at the same time.

She didn't know what to do. She couldn't tell her boss. She was afraid to ask Anderson and Lancer. She sat down and let the situation wash over her. All the connections kept coming. She couldn't stop them. Her mind was full of leads and ideas. She felt like she had tapped into something much greater than herself. It scared her. She was in this now till the end.

36

DAX SAT AT THE BEDSIDE OF A NEWLY ACQUIRED SOUL; HER BODY WAS still warm. He had slid her boyfriend the same concoction he gave her and sent him for a walk. She lay naked under the blanket, lips dark blue, eyes still open. He loved to watch them go. They seemed to linger there in the room with him for a time. He was jealous of their freedom. He knew his time would come.

He stood up and slid the pipe out of her hand. He took one last look around as he made his way to the door. "Jena is such a pretty name," he said as he opened the door and stepped out into the hallway. Nobody ever saw him; nobody noticed anything around there. On his way down the stairs, he stepped over the body of her boyfriend. His eyes were open too. Dax winked at him.

When he got out front, the police were there, moving some vagrants off the block. Dax avoided eye contact and limped his way down the street, his heart pounding in his ears. *That was close,* he thought as he made his way back home. He thought every siren he heard after that was coming for him. It never got old, the fear. Only now he couldn't live without it.

The first time you kill someone is terrifying, but the first time you get away with it is divine. The heavens seem to open and present you with your purpose in life. All that fear turns into elation. Dax's feet lifted from the ground, and he floated home. Away from the pain, away from his petty differences, he coasted the streets of the Downtown Eastside. The landscape came at him in vivid colors: purple, indigo, and green. All the tragedy and pain, was transformed. He was fixing this place, one twisted soul at a time.

37

CASSIDY JUST KEPT DIGGING, *WHAT ELSE COULD SHE DO?* SHE THOUGHT. She couldn't tell anyone because she didn't know how they would respond. Would they help her or shut her down? She couldn't know for sure. All she knew was that she was going to follow this thread down to the end of the line. She started to cross reference shootings with overdose episodes of epic proportions.

In 2012, there was a police shooting of a notorious pimp and pusher named Sam Rightman. The following welfare day (four days later), there was twelve overdose deaths and dozens of overdoses across the city. In 2011, there was a shooting of Marco Perez, a known drug smuggler and rapist. Seven days later on welfare day, the third Wednesday of the month, fifteen people died in one day from overdoses, and there were countless other overdose episodes across the city. In 2010, the same thing happened not once, but twice; two men were killed, and two more bad dope "mardi gras" were reported.

All the while, 80% of police shootings downtown involved people that were either on the waiting list to get into mental health supportive housing or had been previously released. Cassidy felt like she had hit the jackpot. She realized that she couldn't be the only person who knows this. *It is so obvious,* she thought.

She also reminded herself that the police only deal with 7% of the population constantly, so it wouldn't surprise anyone else either if the people they dealt with on a regular basis were being shot. She thought about the doctor's office and the hotels and cringed. *It's like they are certifying them to die,* she thought. The waves of overdoses intrigued her as well. She almost had to admire it. They lose a man and then they take advantage of an overdose holiday – "welfare day". She knew that at least five people die every welfare day, and it wouldn't be a stretch to assume there could be more. They were using historical markers to administer retribution. This was calculated randomness. The last wave of overdoses was October 17, a week after the shooting on "welfare day".

Unbelievable, she thought. She had to tell someone. But who?

38

CASSIDY CLIMBED INTO THE CRUISER A COUPLE WEEKS LATER, FEELING apprehensive. She didn't want to know what she knew. She exchanged the cordial banter with the officers and watched the blocks go by out the window. It was November now, and the streets were tightening up. The rain was torrential at times, but it seemed to wash the streets clean with a depressing gray tranquility. No one wanted to be caught out in it, but once it was underway, you could immediately see the old city come out in full bloom.

Vancouver itself is not a beautiful city. It's in a beautiful place, but it's a mismatch of failed ideas and too much new and old construction mixed together. It's a glass city on the one hand, and an old fur-trading port on the other. But when it rained, it revealed the splendour hiding underneath it.

Cassidy stared out at the rain and started in with her line of questioning. "So, I've been going over the shootings in the last five years, and you guys are dead on when it comes to the deceased being people on mental health assistance."

The two were silent in response. It was as if they were waiting for something; maybe being a cop relinquishes the ability to be surprised because all you see is the inverse of society that nobody else sees.

Cassidy leaned forward and said finally, "The other shootings are interesting as well."

The two shifted quickly in their seats. "Come out with it," Anderson answered back.

"Do you guys want to tell me about them?" she asked.

"We should get medals for those scumbags," Lancer reported.

"Let me ask in another way. Did you notice anything strange about the two shootings that weren't a mental health section 28?" she asked.

"Stop being so cryptic. Those dudes were lifers, scumbags, garbage men," Anderson scoffed.

"What's a garbage man?" Cassidy asked.

"In this line of work, the desperate and vulnerable attract the sharks," Lancer added.

"Killers?" Cassidy asked.

"Worse. You actually have to have a soul to kill. These men don't kill, they devour the helpless like sharks in a feeding frenzy," Anderson finished.

"You know about these men?" Cassidy asked.

"You can't do this job without firsthand knowledge of these kinds of men. It's the curse of the job; the sight of the dead after these men have had their way stays with you forever. I still know guys who are on leave after that pig farm in 2002," Lancer said.

"Do you think they are connected?" Cassidy asked.

"Sometimes these guys work together, and God knows it's a small world, so I wouldn't be surprised if there was at least a mutual ideology between them," Anderson answered.

"Do you think they could coordinate mass overdose episodes?" Cassidy said, inching closer to her motive.

"Like the other day, you mean?" Lancer asked.

"Yes, exactly," Cassidy said triumphantly.

"Never happen. It's the toxic drug supply that's killing these junkies. We've been down this road with pathologists, coroners, doctors, you name it. There is no way these waves are deliberate," Anderson returned.

"Have you looked at the dates of these mass overdose events?" Cassidy asked naively losing momentum.

"What about it?" Lancer demanded.

"They are within a week of the shootings," Cassidy said in a quieter tone; being overwhelmingly right was not something she thought she was all of a sudden.

"Both of them?" Anderson asked.

"All of them," Cassidy answered.

"They were on welfare day, for Christ's sake. Do you know what the overdose rate is during Mardi Gras? It's up 80%," Lancer fired back.

"They are using welfare day to hide their crimes and get retribution," Cassidy said swallowing hard and waiting for the return. She didn't get one. The two just sat up there in the front seat and caught their composure.

"So, what you are saying is that these scumbags are connected, and every time we kill one of them, they poison the population with bad dope?" Anderson asked.

"More or less," Cassidy answered with trepidation in her voice, but with a sense of confidence too.

"You know that whoever did that would have to have complete control of the drug trade in the lower mainland, there are many crews, many hired hands across many boroughs," Lancer stated.

"I don't know about that. All I know is that the dates line up as far back as I can go. It's not perfect, but a pattern is there," Cassidy reassured.

"It's thin at best," Anderson said skeptically.

Cassidy got dropped off shortly after that, and her hands couldn't stop shaking. She had never had a real story before. She had seen them and dreamed about them, but she had never been near one. She was scared to be informing them of something; she felt exposed like she could be killed for knowing it. She went home and locked the door. She looked out the window at a city she thought she knew so well and saw the ugliness of it. The pavement was starting to dry outside after the rain, and she saw the transformation take place. The city was washed, but not cleansed. She didn't know if it would ever be for her now.

39

ANDERSON SAT ACROSS THE TABLE FROM A YOUNG MAN WHO HAD BLACK face paint smudged all over his face. He had been painted up like a skeleton when he tried to rob the Royal Bank earlier that morning. He got farther than most before he was picked up. The cameras left over from the Olympics made sure of that. He sat there staring forlornly at Anderson.

"Well, we can send you back to Kent or you can give us something to make us change our minds," Anderson said like she had said it a thousand times.

He looked her up and down and said, "Fuck off, cunt."

Anderson took a deep breath and opened the file in front of her. "This is your fourth bust in ten years, Eric. You are going down below for a long time unless you help us. The next time you see daylight, you will be in your fifties," Anderson said, levelling with him.

Eric got a gleam in his eye and said, "I hear you guys got a hell of an overdose problem in the city – bad dope they say" Eric said wiping his nose.

"Are you a concerned citizen, Eric?" Anderson returned, adjusting her baseball cap.

"I might be."

"What do you know joe?" Anderson said, extending her arm out across the table like she was consulting a crystal ball.

"I know that dope was no joke; it wasn't no accident either," Eric said looking off at the mirror.

"What does that mean?" Anderson demanded

"I know people who were tipped off before not to touch it, to push it, but not touch it," Eric answered.

Anderson looked at the mirror now too, at Lancer, who she knew was sitting behind it. "Who tipped 'em?" Anderson pressed.

"A man named Saul," Eric said.

"And where can we find him?" Anderson continued.

"You can find the man at the River Rock Hotel most days. Now can I get a cigarette and a coffee?" Eric retorted.

"Sure thing," Anderson responded, closing the file in front of her with a smile.

40

SAUL BERGMAN WAS A SMALL-TIME BOOKIE AND LOAN SHARK THAT HUNG around the River Rock Hotel and Casino amongst other gambling establishments in Richmond. He wasn't hard to find. Anderson and Lancer waited for him in the lobby as he crossed the crosswalk to the hotel. The man was hard to miss; at five foot six and three hundred pounds. He was about fifty-five years old and carried with him the sports page under one arm and a briefcase in his hand.

Anderson walked up to him as he caught his breath coming in the door.

"Hey there, Saul, got a minute?" Anderson said, patting him on the back.

"Not particularly. What do you want," he asked, patting his forehead with a handkerchief that was tightly gripped in one palm.

"Well, to start with, I would like to have a chat with you about your fourteen-year-old niece staying in your room," Anderson said very cordially.

Saul's eyes got more compliant after that. "What can I help you with?"

"Let's go somewhere private," Anderson said leading Saul into the theatre of the hotel with Lancer trailing behind. When they got into the theatre, Saul sat down in one of the theatre seats, and Anderson sat on the back of one of the seats further down in another aisle. Lancer was by the door to make sure nobody came in. It was dark in the theatre. The only light came from the running lights in the aisles and the red exit signs over the doors at the front and back.

"I hear you are quite the man to beat around here," Anderson said crossing her arms.

"I don't know what that means," he said, still wiping sweat from his brow.

"It means that your services around here have not gone unnoticed – first by various sources, and not to mention, the myriad of cameras in this facility."

"Your point?" he said.

"My point is, with the testimony of your niece up there, who we are sending back to her parents in the Okanagan after this, and all we know about old Saul, I think by mid-afternoon today, you can trade in that suit for orange coveralls and a toothbrush," Anderson stated.

"Unless…" Saul said abruptly.

"Unless you tell us everything you know about the last string of overdoses," Lancer said from the door.

Saul sat there for a moment and weighed his options. Finally, he took a deep breath and said, "I know a lot of girls who run dope into Surrey and Richmond. You can say we have an understanding. One of those girls delivers dope here. When she got here, she told me not to let anyone touch the dope, move it only. She said it was red death."

"What's red death?" Anderson asked.

Saul put one hand up and ran it across his neck, "It's a hotshot."

"Why would a hot shot be distributed to the public? Hotshots are used for specific targets," Lancer said.

"Because everyone is the target," Saul said under his breath.

"What?" Anderson pressed.

"Listen, all I know is one of theirs went down, and when that happens, everyone pays. Now I'm a businessman, can I go and conduct my business?" Saul asked.

"Who are these people?" Anderson asked.

"The question you should be asking is: Who aren't these people?" Saul said standing up.

Lancer came up behind him immediately and shoved him back down into his seat. "Who are they?" Lancer demanded, stepping back to the door.

"These men run dope and girls. That's all I know. When they got grief, everybody pays, if you haven't noticed," Saul said, putting his briefcase on his lap and resting his forehead on it.

"What's that supposed to mean?" Anderson pressed.

"Do you really think waves of toxic dope go out over the population without being sanctioned by someone? What business do you know kills its customers on purpose?" Saul said with an air of indifference. "If the slaughterhouse kills a bunch of its customers, they do a massive recall and try to fix the mistake. Nobody recalls this dope. Nobody is trying to fix anything," Saul finished.

"Who are *they*?" Lancer said again sternly.

"Follow the money. You'd be amazed on where it ends up," Saul said with a laugh. "Can I go?" he asked again after a moment.

Anderson nodded to him and then looked over at Lancer. Cassidy was right, and they both knew it. Lancer opened the door for Saul and said, "Catch you later."

The two officers stared at each other for a moment after "remember the first time we came here?" Anderson asked

"Yep, you were married then," Lancer returned.

"Well, I'm not married anymore," she said with a smirk.

"Nope," Lancer said opening the door for her.

The two began cross-referencing overdose incidents as far back as 2000. Out of their own ignorance, they would work diligently now to right a mistake, and all of the lower mainland was about to be turned over to right it.

41

SAUL BERGMAN WAS FOUND DEAD IN THE RIVER ROCK HOTEL TWO DAYS later. He was discovered naked in his bathroom; he had overdosed sometime during the night. It was obvious from the state of the room that he wasn't alone. Anderson and Lancer were called immediately after he was found. The two rushed over. "What the fuck?" Lancer said to Anderson as they stood over the body in the bathroom.

"They work quickly," Anderson said.

Just then, they were interrupted by homicide detectives coming through the door. "Hey" was all that was said between the two groups. "It's a little cramped in here, so if you aren't part of the solution, please get out," was the other thing said.

Lancer and Anderson gunned off the detectives on the way out. "Speaking of ex-husbands," Lancer said to Anderson teasing her.

"He hates you worse than me," she said back to him.

"Seriously, what the fuck was that in there? Who are these people?" Anderson said.

"Let's start with following Saul's money around here, and then see if we can trace it downtown. He must be paying these guys somehow," Lancer returned.

The two got in the car and tapped into the River Rock Casino cameras. A girl and a man with hoods and glasses were seen leaving Saul's room. They got on the SkyTrain, but were lost around Commercial Drive. Comings and goings of Saul Bergman were pretty interesting in the weeks leading up to his death. Cameras have him having lunch in the buffet with an MLA, a few lawyers, and a man that Anderson and

Lancer knew emphatically: the leader of a prominent crime family here in Richmond, Johnny Chu.

Following the money meant just that. With money, you don't get a lot of dirt; you get a lot of discouragement. Everyone knows that these worlds connect somewhere. BC's trade in marijuana was evidence of that alone. Could they tie this world to that of the Downtown Eastside? They knew they couldn't. What they could do was to track the money back to the source of the dope, hopefully. Maybe they could get an arrest and turn somebody up against their bosses. Lancer and Anderson knew that in this city, if they started turning over rocks, before they knew it, they would be running into cops. They wanted to find these killers and try to stay out of the politics.

42

CASSIDY WOKE UP IN DEREK'S BED TO THE SUN SHINING THROUGH THE window. He lived on the twentieth floor of a new building in Yale Town. The view was spectacular. She could see the ocean and the mountains surrounding the city. The sun lit the glass city up to a shine in the morning of reds and yellows; it was breathtaking.

As she was admiring the view, Derek came into the bedroom with a cup of coffee. He was wearing his suit without a tie on. "Here you go. Stay as long as you want and don't worry about cleaning up. I have a service that comes in twice a week," he said as he stood in front of a full-size mirror, tying his tie.

Cassidy watched him closely and hid the lower part of her face in the blankets. She didn't want him to see her jaw, which had completely dropped in awe of this sight. She adored him, probably even loved him, but none of those things anyone needed to know right now. She watched him finish tying the tie, and then he came over to the bed, removed the blanket from over her mouth, and kissed her deeply. "Have a good day," he said as he walked out the door.

Cassidy was speechless. She lay there for a short time and marveled at her existence. Could it be at that altitude she was in heaven? She couldn't know for sure. She got up and took a shower in a massive bathroom with a jacuzzi tub and a standing double shower with two shower heads on either end of it.

Is this marble? she thought, running her hand across it.

When she finished, she walked across the apartment in a white towel bathrobe drinking her coffee. The guy had a hairdryer built into the wall! She was impressed. She thought about her day ahead and how she would stay away from the office; maybe she would take a walk and go for breakfast somewhere. It looked like a beautiful day outside, even in November. She left shortly after that. She took a long look as she walked out of the apartment and took a deep breath. She loved the smell of hardwood floors. As she headed down in the elevator, she was reminded of their first kiss in the elevator on the way down from the revolving restaurant. She floated through the lobby and out into the street.

 Cassidy found a bakery nearby and got a croissant and a coffee. She sat there and took it all in, people rushing around getting to work in dress clothes. This was Vancouver's elite. She admired the similarities and noted tiny differences. The cars were all brand new and the wardrobes spotless, but the people were hurried and balancing kids and coffee the same as in her neighborhood. She was glad she didn't have their lives, regardless of where they lived. She sipped her coffee and became a tourist. She looked up at the buildings and tried to figure out which one was Derek's. She couldn't guess. Was it that one? No, maybe that one.

 After that, she just started walking, past the Library Square Public House, past the Gastown Steam Clock, and then she found herself staring down that long road to the Downtown Eastside. Something was pulling her down there. She began to walk towards it. The cities beauty and lustre began to fade with every tarp and tent she saw in the alleyways and streets she crossed. She eventually ended up at Pigeon Park where all the suffering in the city accumulated into crowds of "hungry ghosts" –people desperate and wandering .

 She saw heavy backpacks and carts. She saw people without shoes, feet black and blistered. She hung her head and took a deep breath of that musty smell that engrossed the breeze that ran through there. The smell of lost souls and death filled the air. Just then, she heard a voice she recognized.

 "Back for some more punishment, I see," she heard from behind her.

She knew the voice by now. It was Clark standing behind her with his cart. He smiled at her as he pressed a bottle of water into her hand and gave her a pat on the shoulder.

"Hey, there," she said, relieved to see a familiar face.

"What brings you down?" he asked, searching her face for signs of life.

"Oh, I'm just out walking around."

"Well, maybe we can walk together."

Just then, a couple started fighting. "Fuck you, goof. I should have left you in '76," the woman yelled as she threw a beer can at a man.

Cassidy was startled by the outburst, but Clark looked at her and said, "True love," and they both laughed. "She must have had too much of a good thing," he said with a chuckle.

Cassidy looked Clark up and down and asked him, "Why do you do this every day? You could easily find a job somewhere, couldn't ya?" Cassidy said watching a man inject himself with heroin leaning up against a wall.

"What? and leave all this?" Clark said with a laugh.

"No seriously, why do you do it?" she asked him.

Clark looked around and took a deep breath. "When I first came here, I was wild. I was just like any of these people, but I was really young too. I was angry and confused. I used drugs, drank, and hurt people. This went on for years until one day I climbed to the top of that building over there, and I was going to jump. I said to the world, "Is this it? Is this all there is?" As I readied myself to jump, I heard the Creator say, "Is this it from you?"

I was startled. I heard the Creator say, "Maybe it's not all about you. There are so many like you; why don't you focus on them? Maybe they have the answers you seek," and he was right. I got off the wheel of trauma and started being of service. I am a leader to my people. I am a guiding voice in the dark," Clark finished and handed a man a T-shirt.

Cassidy looked around at all the suffering and said, "It doesn't seem to end though. It's getting worse."

Clark looked at her and said, "I have no control over the waves. I only control the paddle and where I steer the boat. The wake and the wave are not my concern."

She walked with him a while past the tent shanties and men sleeping on the pavement face down. They walked past the hookers and the pimps, passed the bread lines and the pharmacies. Clark shook people's hands and gave them what he had. He sent people to services, handed out vouchers, and left people in a better state than he found them.

"Aren't you scared ever?" she asked as she watched a man walk up to her wearing a red cellophane mask, look her in the eyes and say, "I've killed, and I'll kill again."

Clark patted him on the shoulder and sent him on his way. "If you respect the forest, the forest will respect you," Clark finished.

Cassidy felt good around him, regardless of the tragedy that unfolded in front of them. She wondered how that could be. She woke up in heaven it seemed, but then she found herself here. This place felt more authentic to her. It didn't need marble; it didn't need a view. It was what it was. It didn't appear to be anything. She was scared of it, but she respected these people more. Their will to survive surpassed any entitlement she witnessed that morning in Yale Town. The people here weren't hiding behind anything, they had no shame.

This was the ultimate paradox hiding in plain sight. How can this place feel more authentic than opulence can look? What was the meaning of life? Aesthetics felt empty to her suddenly. There was life here hiding behind the tragedy – a life-giving substance. She felt rejuvenated by it at first, but she was also repulsed by it. The alchemy of pain and survival was a potent elixir to her. She was on the edge of life and death. People here could go at any minute. They weren't balancing careers and responsibilities, and pretending death didn't exist. They faced it and accepted it. They flaunted it. The average person wouldn't last fifteen minutes down here with street feet. This place held its own opulence; it was in the glossy eyes of the hungry ghosts. The palace was on the inside.

43

THE THING ABOUT VIDEO SURVEILLANCE IS, IF YOU GO BACK FAR ENOUGH, you can usually hit the jackpot. The River Rock Casino holds many jackpots, but none paid as heavy for Lancer and Anderson as the camera in Saul's hallway. A woman walked down that hallway, holding the fourteen-year-old's hand a couple weeks back. The pair recognized the woman. "Is that?" Anderson said nearly jumping from her seat.

"Yep," Lancer returned.

The woman's name was Trixy, and she had a long history going back decades. Trixy was a high-end escort in the 90s; some say she was a model in Paris when she was just thirteen years old. Now in her late thirties, she showed no signs of age except the track marks on her arms. And there she was, plain as day, delivering a girl to Saul's room. Priceless. The two knew where she worked and who she worked for.

If the last two weeks of footage from that hotel had told them anything, it was that this thing went up, way up. Trixy worked for the Chinese mob. She was a madam, and she worked out of Richmond exclusively. The girl came from downtown. She had said she lived on Burrard. These syndicates got girls from all over and they paid a high price. Who they paid and how much was always a mystery, but the two knew this could lead them to the hot dose coming out of the Downtown Eastside.

44

"YOU HEAR ABOUT THE FAT MAN?" DAX ASKED TEX THE NEXT TIME THEIR paths crossed. "Heard he met with an accident," Dax followed.

"Well, you know how it is, if a man starts talking, he usually talks himself out," Tex said, adjusting his coat and staring in the mirror. "Lost the girl, though," Tex said, looking over at Dax.

"Fuck," Dax answered.

"Not easy to come by," Tex redirected.

"Well, at least nobody came knocking at our door," Dax reassured.

"Yeah, not yet," Tex answered. The two idled for a few more moments, and then Tex headed out the door. "Have the bags ready just in case," he said as he left.

Dax nodded. If it's one thing Dax knew, it was that when they come looking, they don't stop. He packed a couple bags and counted rolls of cash. The truck was in storage, and it was only six blocks away. They could be gone in a heartbeat.

45

TRIXY, AKA MONIQUE TOUSSAINT, EMIGRATED FROM FRANCE WHEN SHE was twenty-five at the end of a very long modeling career that started at thirteen. She was quickly absorbed into the high-price escort business and rose to the top to become a madam in a tri-owned fantasy business the Chinese mob was running out of Richmond.

Anderson and Lancer caught up to her coming out of a brothel on Robson. "I thought you hussies never left the airport," Anderson said with a smile.

Trixy looked over at Anderson and said, "Well, it surprises me you don't know. You would have been a cash register girl," Trixy shot back at her. Trixy took in the field and scanned for exits as she acted whimsically "Am I under arrest? Or do you two just want a taste, just like the rest of your lot?" she said clearing the hair from her eyes and running her left hand up her thigh checking her stockings.

"We got something to show you, get in," Lancer said, opening the car door.

"Oh, he does speak. Not just the muscle after all," Trixy said, rolling her eyes and slowly lowering herself into the car.

"Is this you?" Anderson said, raising her tablet up so Trixy could see the footage from the backseat. It was undeniable; the lighting in the video was impeccable.

"Just escorting a woman across town and into a safe place. No law against that," Trixy said, looking out the window.

"There's laws against murder though," Lancer interjected.

"What murder?" Trixy shot back forcefully.

"Saul Bergman," Anderson responded.

"Fuck off," Trixy said flippantly.

"We got a fourteen-year-old girl in custody that will cop to it all," Lancer returned.

"I had never met that girl before. I found her at the SkyTrain and decided to give her a safe place to stay," Trixy said nonchalantly.

"Saul Bergman was a safe place?" Anderson said dismissively.

"Hey, a luxury hotel and an older man was the best that girl could hope for, trust me," Trixy said, lighting a smoke.

"You can't smoke back there," Lancer said.

"Then pull over top cop, and let me out," Trixy fired back at him.

"Why do you say that about the girl?" Anderson pressed.

"Like I have to tell you," Trixy said, looking Anderson in the eye.

"Where did she come from? For real?" Anderson asked again.

"Downtown," Trixy said reluctantly.

"Where?" Anderson pressed.

"What do I get? Does this look like a charity I'm running?" she said nonchalantly, butting her cigarette while she looked at Lancer in the rear-view mirror.

"How about we let you go, and forget about you?" Anderson proposed.

"That's a start," Trixy answered.

"Listen, when we start investigating, we will leave your name out of it, or we can go downtown, and we can show you off down there driving around with us," Anderson finished.

"I got her from Carrall Street. There's a warehouse with a basement at East Cordova. Be careful," Trixy said with fear in her voice.

Anderson and Lancer dropped her at the SkyTrain after that. Nobody waved goodbye.

46

SURVEILLANCE WAS SET UP ON THE CORNER OF EAST CORDOVA AND Carrall; two crews rotated in twelve-hour shifts. They didn't find anything. In their spare time, they watched traffic flows in and out of Pigeon Park, hoping to get something there. After a couple weeks of this, they were forced to watch the site themselves.

"You know she could have been lying," Lancer said, breaking the silence.

"You think I haven't thought of that?" Anderson returned quickly.

"Look at this place, it's like the night of the living dead. All the traffic from Pigeon, construction, and café traffic. Hard to find a needle in a haystack here," Lancer said with skepticism.

"You ever hear about all that talk back in the day about tunnels under the city?" Anderson asked him.

"Yeah, but it was all discredited. The only real tunnels were up near the clock or that post office tunnel, not to mention the UBC tunnels," Lancer answered while yawning.

"We are near Water Street, and they definitely had tunnels," Anderson returned.

"What do you want to do? Pull the sewer main and go in after the ninja turtles?" Lancer scoffed.

"Something, I know there's something here," Anderson said, refusing to give up.

"Not without a bulldozer and a spotlight. It's all mud down there around Chinatown. The holes would fill with water," Lancer said dismissively.

"This isn't Chinatown. This is down from Water Street. There are tunnels leading to the water here, I know it," Anderson urged.

"Let it go," Lancer said forcefully. Lancer turned on the ignition and drove off. Anderson gave the corner one last pass with her eye, and in that moment, she saw a huge rat run into the side of a wall off Carrall.

"Stop the car," she yelled.

"What?" Lancer pleaded.

"I said stop the fucking car," Anderson said as she jumped out and ran up to the wall. She looked the building up and down and then ran back to the car. "212. Remember that," she said as they drove down the street. "Go to the public works office," Anderson demanded.

"What the fuck?" Lancer said in protest. "I just want to see what the pipes look like down there is all, then we can go follow some other lead, okay?" she finished.

"Whatever," Lancer said as he drove downtown.

47

CASSIDY DECIDED TO GO BACK TO WORK AFTER A SMALL HIATUS. SHE WAS greeted by some, but her editor wasn't happy about her missing her ride-alongs.

"What am I paying you for?" is what he said. She quickly agreed to meet with the officers the day after next. She spent the rest of the day doing background into applications filed with mental health. There was anywhere between a thousand applications to three thousand at any one time.

How could there be so many? she thought. *She thought she would go ask somebody.*

She looked up a psychiatrist they had done a story on a while back named Dr. Roseman. He was against the medicalization of mental health services and spoke out about it publicly. She called his office and got an interview with him later that day. She spent the rest of the day prepping questions and reading reports about standoffs with police involving Section 28, the Mental Health Act used to detain people suffering from psychosis.

Report after report, the files looked the same. The victim was brandishing a weapon of some sort in a delusional state; the officers opened fire. Cassidy thought back to the first ride-along with Lancer and Anderson and how they disarmed a man by talking to him. She thought about her editors and how they thought that kind of story presented the wrong picture. She packed her stuff and headed to the offices of Dr. Roseman shortly after that.

When Cassidy got to Roseman's office they were packing up for the day. Cassidy was shown into his office and told to wait. A few moments later, a relatively old man walked into the room reading a chart. He was early sixties with gray hair and penny loafer shoes. He was wearing a blue sweater, and tanned khaki pants. He looked up from his reading and said, "Good day, I'm Dr. Roseman. How may I help you?"

Cassidy looked into the man's grayish-blue eyes and said, "I'm here to get your take on the closing of the Riverview Hospital and the increase in Section 28 shootings in the Downtown Eastside. She prepared for a deflection or an oratory on public safety, but what she got was quite unexpected. "The Riverview is just a continuation of the pharmaceutical industries attempt to medicalize the human experience. The shootings are a direct response to the pills making people crazy." He said so nonchalantly it made Cassidy's jaw drop.

"How's that?" Cassidy asked fumbling for her cell phone to record the audio. "It's simple really. Schizophrenia used to have less symptoms and could be completely cured within a year if the person had been showing symptoms for only a year or so. In fact, 85% of people would come back symptom-free. The person was sent to a farm outside the place that caused the illness. You see, these illnesses come from the environment. A person can be cured of them if they are not exacerbated by pills and stress, like they are now," he said.

"Do you mind if I record this?" she asked.

"Sure, but it won't make a bit of difference though," he said.

"Why?" she asked. "I've said this before and obviously it's in all the journals going back to the beginning of the magic pill in the 50s," he answered.

"Let's let the readers be the judge of that," Cassidy said reassuringly.

Roseman looked at her with a smile and then went into something he had said a thousand times. "There is no such thing as a chemical imbalance in patients. Let's start there. The pills raised serotonin levels, so it was assumed that having low serotonin levels was indicative of depression, but that's not true. Control groups showed that people who had low serotonin levels were no less depressed than people with high levels, but that's not what was told to patients. The studies never went past twelve weeks. If they had, you would see that the longer they stayed on the pills, the worse their symptoms would get."

Cassidy's eyes went wide, and she said, "What?"

"Yeah, the pills make your cells misfire, stall, and mutate. The long-term effects of the pills are so devastating that it would be better in all cases if you never took them at all," he said, sitting down as if defeated by his own statement.

"So, the closing of Riverview makes this worse?" Cassidy asked.

"Of course, it does. Now you have people living in ghettos, addicted to pills that are making them crazy. No wonder they are being killed by police. Taking that poison unsupervised in a ghetto is a recipe for disaster," he answered.

"People know about this?" Cassidy asked.

"People have known about this for decades – since Vicodin, for Christ sake. Then it was barbiturates, now its benzodiazepines that have already been outlawed in the states, OxyContin, fentanyl, and so many more antipsychotics and antidepressants," he said.

Cassidy looked across the desk in horror. She just couldn't believe that this was happening. She thought this was just some doctor's downtown who were taking advantage of poor people, not the whole medical system. "So, you say that the pharmaceutical industry has taken over mental health?" Cassidy asked to clarify.

"It's all about lobbying the government. The government sees what it pays for in patient programs and then it is presented with an outpatient program that works with pills and keeps people in the community. The government chooses the outpatient program to save money, and the pharmaceutical industry comes in with the pills. Now you can see what keeping all those people in the city looks like – just go down to the Downtown Eastside. Those people are left there to explode into a litany of mental health identifiers and eventually, like you say, they either die of an overdose, get killed by police, or worse."

"Or worse?" Cassidy asked.

Dr. Roseman looked over at her and then just said what he had always held back, "Or they are killed by the men that control Carrall Street."

"What men?" Cassidy asked.

"I had a patient once who told me there is a group of men that work off Hastings and Carrall dispatching souls they deem worthy of death. They kidnap women and sell them into the human trafficking market. They feed on the pain and opportunity down there," he said wiping the perspiration from his forehead and leaning back in his chair.

Cassidy looked back at him in disillusionment.

"What is the answer then?" Cassidy asked just to get some traction.

"These people need to be taken off the substances or, at best, never be put on them. They need a place to go outside the environment to figure it out for themselves with people who want to see them self-actualize. Not like now, where people want to prescribe them out of the job market and leave them in ghettos to die both figuratively and actually. Every time you designate someone as 'special' with no evidence, you deem them unfit. You take their spirit away, their will to live. It's like you have killed them already. They become what they are labelled, and then they die horrible deaths, many before their heart stops beating," Roseman finished with a sigh.

Cassidy stopped recording and thanked him for his time. She left sometime after that. She walked out into a world she saw for the first time. A world built on a lie. A world dying to hear something that was true.

48

ANDERSON PARKED OUTSIDE THE CITY PLANNERS BUILDING AND HEADED in.

"I'm going to find a bathroom and some lunch," Lancer said, walking down the street.

She didn't need him anyway, she thought. Her dad had been an architect. She used to go to work with him on the weekends to give her mom a break. She knew how to read blueprints. When she got inside, she pulled building permits and blueprints going back fifty years. She was just about to find another angle when she saw it. The block they were watching at East Cordova and Carrall used to have a butcher shop. It was right down from Blood Alley, the meat district, where they used to just throw the blood out in the street, giving it the name.

To the other side of Carrall was a holding facility and auction house. It used to be one building stretching from Powell and Columbia all the way down to East Cordova. It has since been subdivided, but the property shares the same basement. The entrance is on Powell and Columbia. She rifled through the blueprints and could see that the basements had been sealed off on the East Cordova side. It was the first and second floor only all the way back to Columbia.

"What the fuck?" Anderson said out loud, alarming some contractors and architects.

"Sorry," she said to them, waving her hand for them to go back to work. Just then Lancer came through the door with a sandwich sticking out of his mouth. She brushed by him, knocking him back into the door.

"What's this?" he cried.

"We are watching the wrong door; the entrance is on Columbia," she said as she raced out to the car so she could get a detail set up on Powell and Columbia.

Lancer jumped in feeling slightly disorientated. "I got you a sandwich, too," he said.

"I can't eat right now. We are on the hunt. I feel this one in my bones," she said, as she pulled out and drove towards the station.

49

WITHIN ONLY TWELVE HOURS, THE INTEL THEY COLLECTED ABOUT AN operation running out of a secret middle door entrance to a basement on Powell and Columbia was astonishing. Pimps, drug runners, and all sorts of day walkers frequented the store on the ground floor, and groups of men would come in and out of the basement at night. They obtained a search warrant and waited for morning. Anderson sat two blocks away with Lancer in the car waiting for tactical to arrive.

"This is it, old man," Anderson said, patting him on the leg.

Lancer laughed. "I like when you get all excited; it's been a while," he said, nudging her with his elbow.

"There's something about real police work that makes me wet," she said tapping the steering wheel. Just then, tactical arrived, Anderson got out and told them to hold tight. They were going in at the first hint of red light on the horizon. She went to the back of her car and grabbed two bullet-proof vests. She threw one in the car at Lancer, and he put his on. They checked their weapons and waited for that red cascade to come on to the horizon. This was it.

"Tactical proceed to the front door. There is an entrance going down into the basement to the left of the door to the shop. What we know is that there is one way in and one way out. We will be on your six, over," Anderson said into the radio.

Her hands began to vibrate as she approached the building behind tactical. They booted in the door and threw tear gas down into the basement. Smoke started to barrel out of the doorway, and then, one by one, tactical went down the stairs screaming, "POLICE! FREEZE!"

Anderson and Lancer eased down into the basement as shots were being fired somewhere below. The two got to the bottom of the stairs and stayed low. It was dark down there, with only a few lights protruding from passage ways that seemed to be going everywhere. They could hear a struggle and more shots.

"Command, we got an officer down. Call the paramedics."

The two eased into the next room through one of the entrances and saw the officer on the ground being attended to and two men bleeding out against the wall in handcuffs. The team went through another doorway. When Anderson and Lancer came through that door, they stopped in their tracks. In front of them stood a number of animal cells with chicken wire.

There were two groups of half-naked bodies huddled at the far end of it, sobbing and screaming. As the smoke started to settle, you could see the faces and the eyes of the bound women searching the officers for answers. One of the officers was pouring water into one of the girl's mouths through the wire while other officers opened the cage with wire cutters. There had to be twelve girls there. Anderson counted them as she made her way back into a bigger room where there were chairs and a TV.

The place was huge. There were tunnels in the walls that lead left and right from the main room they were in. There was a bathroom in one, and a lab in the other with kilos of product wrapped up in cellophane. Towards the back, there was a locked room where the lock needed to be broken off. In that room was a dead body, skinned and hung like deer. Anderson threw up on the floor at the site of it. Lancer patted her on the back.

She could hear the paramedics coming in, and she went out the way they came in, to the street. When she got out there, she was disgusted. "Fuckin' animals," she said to herself as she took control of the scene.

"Block these streets and get homicide and forensics down here," she said to the patrolmen standing guard.

They kicked in the front door of the store and found more dope and cash. The bust was a huge success. They got forty-eight kilos of pure fentanyl, twenty of crystal meth, and a host of other substances they sent down to the lab. There was two million dollars in cash. Homicide was doing DNA tests on the body. Immigration and missing persons were cross referencing the women. Anderson stood across the street and sipped on her coffee as she watched the drama unfold.

"The chief is coming down. We are getting medals," Lancer said, walking up to her and leaning against the wall.

"I bet," she said spitting out into the street.

"Something doesn't feel right," she said.

"The two guys inside?" Lancer said.

"Yeah, we should have gathered more intel. This seems so much bigger than this," Anderson said with regret.

"Feels like the pig farm. Remember that?" Lancer said to her.

"Could I ever forget?" she shot back at him.

The two sat there for a moment after, and it was bittersweet. They knew there was more, but there always is. It would take them a while to come back to equilibrium. They had saved some lives and prevented even more from falling prey to these animals in the months to come. The thirst was unquenchable for justice when it comes to this sort of thing unfortunately. Part of the job. Tomorrow was another day.

50

"HOW COME YOU DIDN'T CATCH THIS? YOU'RE IN A CAR WITH THESE TWO for months, and you miss out on the scoop of the decade?" Cassidy's editor yelled at her.

She looked shocked. She had watched the news that morning and marveled at the carnage and the insinuation that this place had been operating for years. She had to read about it just like everybody else. She called Anderson, but nobody got back to her. She decided it was time to write her story. The spotlight was on the Downtown Eastside, and she wasn't going to waste it. She gathered her notes and went to a rival publication for the pitch. When she got there, they ushered her into the back room, so nobody saw her, and she gave them the pitch. The title of the report would read: "Police Used as Executioners to Rid the Streets of the City's Self-Made, Mental Health Crisis." She was given an advance and offered a freelance job after that. She set herself to writing.

51

A MACK TRUCK DROVE OUT OF THE CITY THAT MORNING WITH TEX IN THE driver's seat and Dax looking out over the city. It was sad to leave her again. They headed to the ferry terminal to Victoria. As Dax climbed out of the truck and steadied himself with his cane, Tex said, "home sweet home for you, boy. David will be waiting for you." Tex said as he revved up the engine and drove away.

    Dax caned his way to the gate and bought a ticket. He made his way up to the walk on platform and watched the ferry approach. He studied the waves of the ocean and took a deep breath. He could see the newspapers in everyone's hand. People were eating up the headlines. "Butchers' Den of Powell Street" one paper read. He took pride in his work and marveled at the popularity of the bust. He stared at the sheep as they read the paper and dreamt of his next kill. He wasn't the same man who had left Victoria; he was going back a king. He would hunt the helpless and dispatch the useless. All he could taste was death, and all he saw was opportunity.

52

CASSIDY SAT AT A COFFEE SHOP SOMEWHERE DOWN OFF GEORGIA, contemplating her options. She was really nervous she had never written anything like this before. This series of articles could make her infamous in the city. Just then, Derek walked in and found her seated towards the back of the room at her own table.

"Hey honey, how's it going?" he asked solemnly.

"Don't ask. I still have stage fright," she answered with a look of dismay.

Since the Butchers' Den case, the city had turned hostile towards the people of the east end. There were more shootings, more incarcerations and way more indifference towards the people down there than ever. This story had to come out, but she didn't know how to begin.

Derek ordered a coffee and then looked at her. "Maybe just start with your experience and work up from there?" he said cautiously.

She looked over at him and nodded, taking a sip of her coffee and closing her computer. "What are you up to today?" she asked, taking a deep breath.

"You know, buy low, sell high," he said with a smile.

She laughed a bit. She had no idea how his business worked. She looked over at him and was grateful for him in her life. Just then she had an idea "how did your dad do it all those years?" she asked out of nowhere.

Derek looked up at her and said, "Nobody believes it, but it's about the people next to you," he said.

"As simple as that?" she asked with a smile.

The Opiate Murders 3

"No, that's the part that gets complicated, because your coworkers are human, and you are following them into hell sometimes. Mistakes will be made, and people will get hurt, but at the end of the day, if you go home alive, you have won. That's what he would say on the worst days, and there were lots of them," he said with a nod of reverence.

"You should have been a preacher," she said with a smile.

"I'm only a cop's son. We are all like this, trust me," he replied, and they both laughed. "I have to go to work now," he said.

"Have a good day, Derek, and thank you." She watched him walk out into the rain and thought about his life, and then she thought about Lancer and Anderson. She opened up her computer and began to type.

> Since the year 2000, there has been a great shift in our city that many people have gradually witnessed. Once upon a time on Hastings Street, every third person wasn't wearing a hospital coat and slippers. There used to be a place where people could go for long-term care. Riverview started being phased out long before it closed its doors in 2012. City planners and doctors gave in to pharmaceutical technicians long ago.
>
> You see, this city had a large part of its budget allocated to mental health, and the city planners wanted to get rid of it. The pharmaceutical reps and lobbyists got together and devised a plan for outpatient care. Outpatient care would see the most vulnerable in our population reside in one-room ghettos on the Downtown Eastside. For years, these people have waited on mental health housing lists, taking toxic cocktails of drugs prescribed to them by doctors in an eight-minute interview at a walk-in clinic.
>
> The patients walking the streets of our city with no refuge fall victim to the crime and violence that plague the lower Downtown Eastside. They live on assistance cheques and eat at homeless shelters. They get addicted to narcotics and sell their bodies. Finally, once the doctor, the psychologist, and pharmacists are done with them, they would be killed by police in a delusional psychosis caused from poor living conditions and toxic prescriptions. The people who end up living in the

slums of the Regent or the Balmoral are good people who just asked for help. They are citizens having a hard time. What they are transformed into and how they are dispatched is a crime against humanity.

Since 1955, reports have shown that SSRI's can cause Akathisia which is a reaction in the liver that causes an enzyme to trigger instantaneous violent outbursts. These outbursts have caused normal people with little to no symptoms of sleeplessness or anxiety to murder their spouses, children, psychiatrists, and coworkers.

The companies who sell these drugs know this. The people of the Downtown Eastside, in most cases, are survivors of child abuse, molestation, and neglect. They are given sometimes eight different prescriptions without a risk stratification. There is no assessment for risk factors. Then they are sent out into the streets to fend for themselves. These people end up in violent confrontations with hallucinations, and then they are killed by police.

Sources inside the police department state that their job is to uphold the law. The law is being broken by these people, and they are putting the public at risk of danger, so police have to respond, but this all starts long before they come into contact with police. It all starts in a doctor's office. It starts in a child's clinical assessment. It starts at home. The idea of the magic pill has been around since penicillin, but the mind is not an infection. The mind is far too complicated to be governed by psychotropic drugs.

The chemical balance theory was started by the drug companies. Because SSRI's raised serotonin levels, it was decided that depression must come from having low serotonin, but studies have shown since the 1970's that it isn't true. Control groups in studies have proved that there was no correlation between depression and low serotonin. In fact, the control groups with low serotonin in some studies were found to be happier and more alert than the groups with high serotonin levels.

So why do we believe it? Drug companies believe it – that's why. The drug companies believe that the problem is within the brain, even though they have never been able to locate the problem there. They promote that you are only one prescription away from happiness. The people deemed mentally ill are being systematically demoralized, dispirited, and then dispatched by the system.

It started with shutting down long-term-care facilities that worked away from the environments that caused these problems. Before 1955, 85% of schizophrenia designations could be cured with one year away on a farm or in an institution. Now the symptoms have been exacerbated, and the treatment is infused with toxic cocktails, so the person is permanently diagnosed out of the workforce and out of their own mind. You find them begging outside of stores in the rain and addicted to drugs.

You see a homeless person with no shoes and nowhere to go, but that person is you or me, after an eight-minute doctor's appointment and self-proclaimed anxiety. The functional impairment that can be caused in a short time on these pills can never be reversed in some cases. People end up not being able to relate to their children or friends anymore. They are isolated from the world from the inside. This is a systematic process that begins at the beginning, not at the end.

These tragedies can be prevented. Instead of treating the effect, you need to reverse the causes. Thousands of people take these prescriptions every day while they are on wait lists for mental health housing. If they weren't on the pills and were sent to an environment where they could heal, they would at least have a fighting chance at living a normal life. Today, they are being sent into a war with themselves against the backdrop of one of the worst ghettos in the country. The Downtown Eastside residents have had enough tragedy for one lifetime. Do they really deserve a never-ending train of new, lost and delusional patients to contend with?

The Butchers' Den case could have been discovered and dispatched years earlier. But because police services are reacting to 130 mental health calls per day, missing persons reports aren't followed up with as quickly as they could be. The police are being overwhelmed by mental health calls, which makes it easier for real crime to go undetected. Our city is taxed with mental health disturbances. In a time when there are thousands of drugs for mental illness, isn't it strange that populations are sicker than they have ever been? Shouldn't all these magic pills be reducing mental illness – not exacerbating it?

The solutions and way forward are not easy. We can start with actual clinical studies by people who aren't employed by the drug companies. We can look at preventative measures like opening up inpatient care facilities outside the city. We can start looking to the real culprits in these police shootings. In law, they look for who set the series of events in motion. The conditions for these shootings were set long ago by people who are not police. When a person is prescribed eight different psychotropic drugs at once, each with books of side effects all interacting within a body that is already nervous, and then placed in a ghetto to live off assistance payments and eat at homeless shelters, the police are not to blame for what they become when they are gunned down. These people were carefully created somewhere else. It's just the police and other emergency services who have to mop them up.

53

ON THE THIRD WEDNESDAY OF THE MONTH, DECEMBER 18, THERE WAS A massive amount of overdose deaths, and they didn't stop. By the end of the week, twenty-five people had died from overdose across the lower mainland, and there were fifteen overdose deaths in Victoria, BC. The combination of the holidays and welfare day were quickly bolstered as the reason for the wave of deaths, but there were two cops in the Downtown Eastside who knew better.

"These fuckin' people are insidious," Anderson said, throwing the radio on the dashboard.

"They are using historical patterns and they are highly organized, Victoria this time," Lancer said as he took a sip of his coffee.

"Maybe the article will do some good," Anderson said.

"Maybe," Lancer responded reluctantly.

54

THE NEW YEAR CAME AND WENT FOR CASSIDY. SHE WAS SET TO PUBLISH her first article as a freelance writer. The year 2014 offered so much promise. She already had a number of articles planned. She read the headlines about the wave of overdoses, and she admired how easily they were dismissed. She hoped to change that. Her first article about mental health patients was coming out this Friday, and she was excited. She had only to send it in.

As Cassidy made her way up to her building, she noticed the front door latch was broken again. She came in and entered her apartment. She looked around and threw her keys on the kitchen table. She took a deep breath and went into her room. As she took off her clothes to take a shower and ran the water to get it to the right temperature, she studied the back of the buildings and their fire escapes. Stepping in, Cassidy let the water flow all over her body and welcomed the cleansing.

She didn't hear the closet in her bedroom open. She didn't see the shadow. As she reached for her conditioner, she was sprayed in the face with a concoction of fentanyl and benzodiazepine. She dropped to her knees instantly and lay there gasping for her last breath with the water flowing over her body. She watched her last moments wash away like the water falling down the drain. She never published her articles. Her laptop was missing from the scene. Lancer and Anderson went through the Downtown Eastside looking for suspects, but they couldn't find any. It was a total mystery.

55

ON NOVEMBER 2, 2014, THE "DAY OF THE DEAD," THERE WAS A PROCESSION of bodies that made their way from the Downtown Eastside to Stanley Park. There were thousands of skeletons with faces painted like death. The police tried to stop them, but they were sieged at every opportunity. Nobody understood where these people came from or what they were doing till they reached the park.

Community leaders from the Downtown Eastside had organized the event to bring awareness to the staggering number of missing women, police shootings, and overdose deaths since 2007. Stanley Park was filled with the families of the victims of the overdose crisis. Candles were distributed, and the park was alive with the shadows of the dead. Traditional Aboriginal groups gave prayers to the Creator for healing while the rest roamed the vigils crying and sharing stories of the fallen angels of the Downtown Eastside.

Somewhere in the darkness, a candle was lit, somewhere in all that darkness Derek had lit a candle for Cassidy and put her picture up with all the others distributed on trees all around the park. He remembered her smile, and the passion she had for people. Tears filled his eyes as he backed away from the tree and was absorbed into the crowds of people twisting and turning in grief. He wasn't alone and in that he felt safe.

Outside the perimeter of the event, stood Anderson. "Listen, you see someone suspicious, you take pictures. You follow any known suspects. This isn't a vigil; it's a perp walk. We know that these animals are here," she finished.

Dozens of police undercover searched the faces of the crowd. Men who were alone or smiling were documented and followed. Lancer stood in front of Cassidy's tree and hung his head in respect. A young man with a cane and a face painted like a skeleton stood next to him. Lancer put his hat back on and walked away. Dax lingered for a moment. So many beautiful souls were here on display; it took everything not to smile.

He couldn't miss this event, he hopped on the first ferry as soon as he heard about it. As he stood there, he was swept away by the crowd circling the trees. He floated there with them, absorbing their grief. He thought back to Amber and how she waited for him there. He prayed for death, so they could be together, but his hunger for souls controlled him now. He had his purpose, and he set himself to it. He headed out of the park and back the way the crowd came. He would catch his next victim on the road back to the east end.

THE END

CPSIA information can be obtained
at www.ICGtesting.com
Printed in the USA
BVHW050618300622
640894BV00001B/35